THE LOST PRINCESS RETURNS

UNCHARTED REALMS – BOOK 6

by

Jeffe Kennedy

A Broken Girl… An Avenging Warrior

More than two decades have gone by since Imperial Princess Jenna, broken in heart and body, fled her brutal marriage—and the land of her birth. She's since become Ivariel: warrior, priestess of Danu, trainer of elephants, wife and mother. Wiser, stronger, happier, Ivariel has been content to live in her new country, to rest her battered self, and to recover from the trauma of what happened to her when she was barely more than a girl.

But magic has returned to the world—abruptly and with frightening force—and Ivariel takes that profound change as a sign that it's time to keep a promise she made to the sisters she left behind. Ivariel must leave the safety she's found and return to face the horrors she fled.

As Ivariel emerges from hiding, she discovers that her vicious brother is now Emperor of Dasnaria, and her much-hated mother, the Dowager Empress Hulda, is aiding him in his reign of terror. Worse, it seems that Hulda's resurrection of the tainted god Deyrr came about as a direct result of Jenna's flight long ago.

It's up to Ivariel—and the girl she stopped being long ago—to defeat the people who cruelly betrayed her, and to finally liberate her sisters. Determined to cleanse her homeland of the evil that nearly destroyed her, Ivariel at last returns to face the past.

But this time, she'll do it on her own terms.

ᴀᴄᴋɴᴏᴡʟᴇᴅɢᴇᴍᴇɴᴛꜱ

Many thanks to Ellie Topitzer, whose comment on Facebook reminded me of Jepp's "prophecy" in *The Edge of the Blade*. That brought together a bunch of threads that needed tying, with perfect serendipity.

As always, thanks to fantastic assistant Carien, for happily reading as soon as I send, and for emergency everything. Much gratitude to Evergreen Lee for proofreading and more! Love to Kelly Robson, who asked about *The Lost Princess* every day, and to Grace Draven, for wisdom and common sense.

To many readers who have loved Ivariel's story and demanded more, many thanks for your gentle persistence and enthusiastic cheering. You all were right: it totally needed to be written.

Ecstatic hand flailing to Ravven for yet another incredible cover. You exactly captured Jenna as grown-up Ivariel. Seriously—looking at this image gives a visceral thrill.

Many thanks to my family, my wonderful friends, and the larger writing community.

Love to David, first, last, and always.

Thank you for reading!

Credits
Line and Copy Editor: Evergreen Lee
Cover: Ravven, ravven.com.

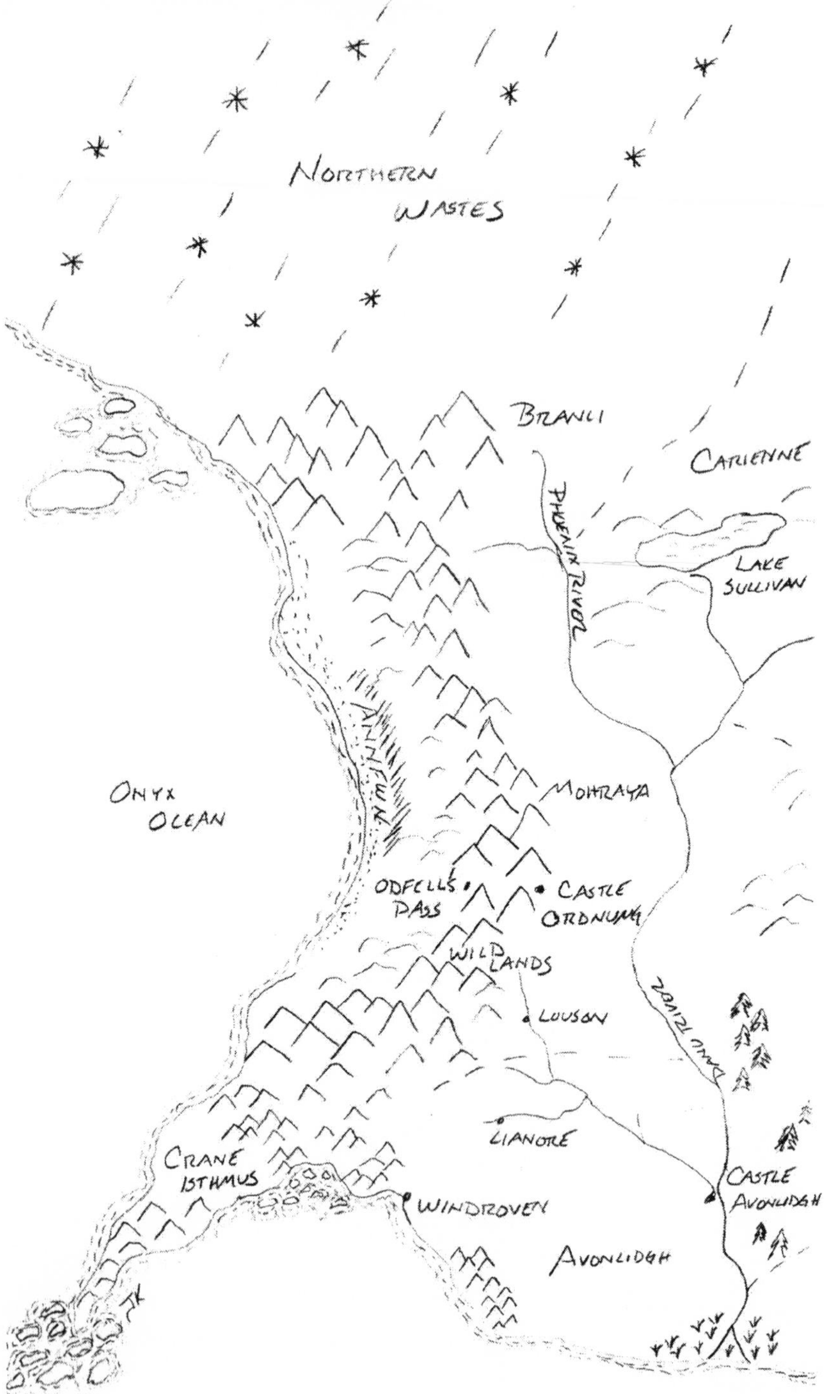
Northern Wastes
Branci
Carienne
Phoenix River
Lake Sullivan
Annfwn
Onyx Ocean
Mohraya
Odfells Pass
Castle Ordnung
Wild Lands
Louson
Danu River
Lianore
Crane Isthmus
Windroven
Castle Avonlidgh
Avonlidgh

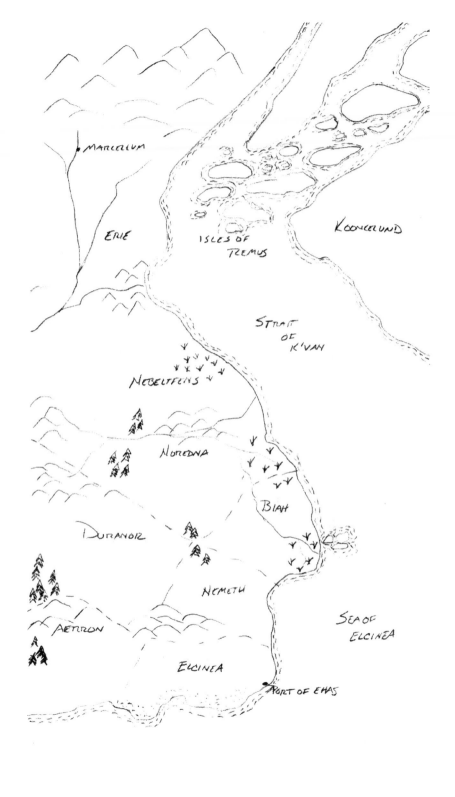

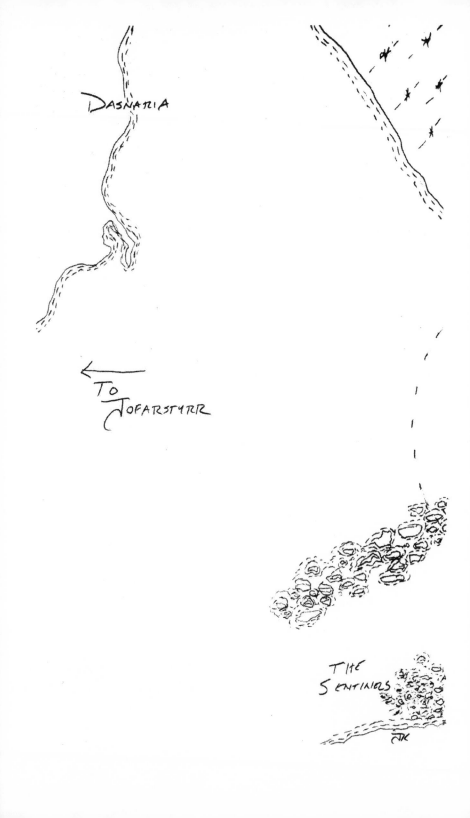

DASNARIA

TO
JOFARSTYRR

THE
SENTINELS

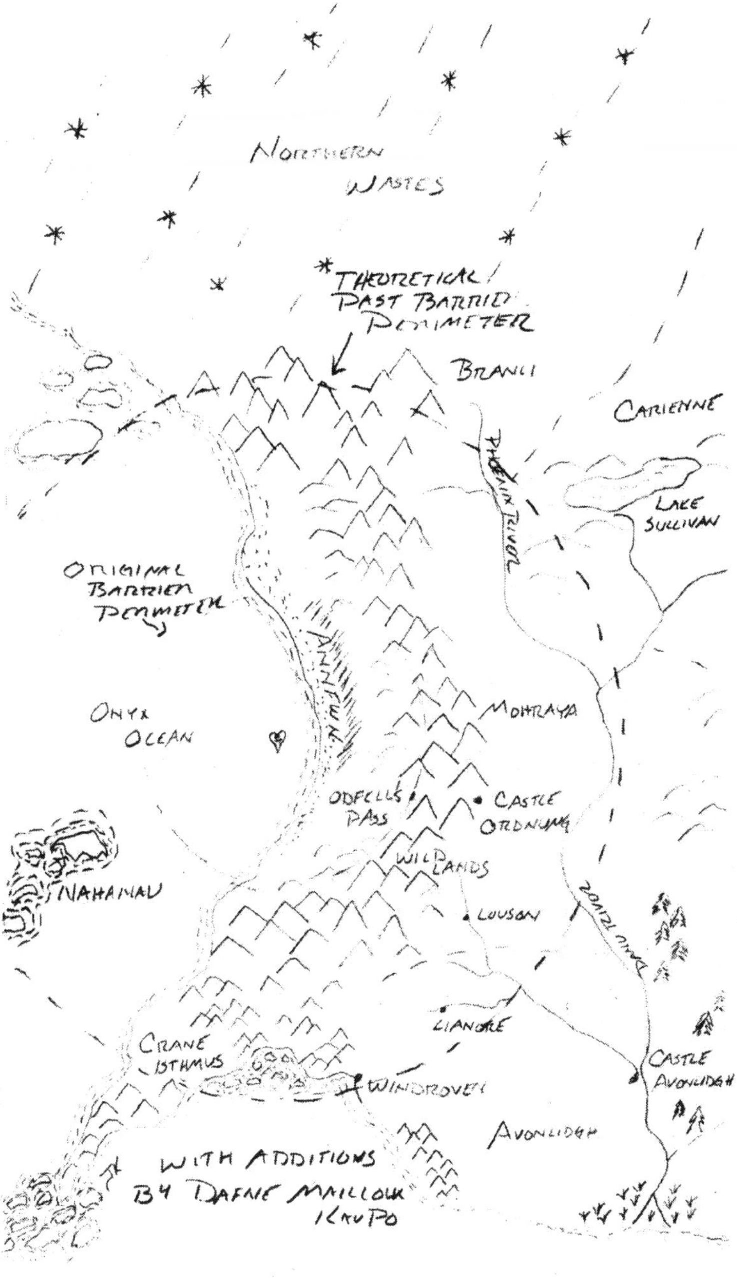
NORTHERN WASTES
THEORETICAL PAST BARRIER PERIMETER
CARIENNE
LAKE SULLIVAN
PHOENIX RIVER
ORIGINAL BARRIER PERIMETER
ONYX OCEAN
MOHRAYA
ODFELLS PASS
CASTLE ORDNUNG
WILDLANDS
LOUSON
NAHANAU
LIANORE
CRANE ISTHMUS
WINDROVEN
CASTLE AVONLIDGH
AVONLIDGH
WITH ADDITIONS BY DAFNE MAILLOUX KAUPO

The Lost Princess Returns

by Jeffe Kennedy

Dear Reader,

The Lost Princess Returns brings together a plot thread that ran through three separate, but (obviously) intertwined stories.

Harlan first appears in *The Talon of the Hawk*, book three of The Twelve Kingdoms trilogy. Jepp also first appears in that book. That trilogy also introduced characters that appear in this book: Ursula, Andi, Rayfe, and Dafne.

The Pages of the Mind, which kicks off The Uncharted Realms series, is Dafne's story, and introduces Kral, Nakoa and Akamai—whose tale is at last tied off here, though not fully told. In book two of The Uncharted Realms, *The Edge of the Blade*, Jepp goes to Dasnaria, meets Inga and Helva, among others, and first learns Jenna's story. A great deal of *The Lost Princess Returns* owes itself to seeds planted in *The Edge of the Blade*. The Uncharted Realms continued with Zynda's book, *The Shift of the Tide*, and Karyn's book, *The Arrows of the Heart*, and culminated in the climactic battle told in *The Fate of the Tala*. There's also a novella, *The Dragons of Summer*, that takes place between *The Arrows of the Heart* and *The Fate of the Tala* that adds some bits of Jenna/Ivariel's story.

The Chronicles of Dasnaria trilogy goes back twenty(ish) years in the past, to tell of Jenna's disastrous first marriage (*Prisoner of the Crown*), her journey to escape and how she becomes Ivariel (*Exile of the Seas*), and her eventual healing (*Warrior of the World*).

So, though we've listed *The Lost Princess Returns* as part of The Uncharted Realms, in many ways it's also the climactic book of The Chronicles of Dasnaria.

A complicated web, I know…

Thanks so much for reading!

~ 1 ~

I GREW UP in paradise.
Or, so I was led to believe.

I've since learned how much of that was a lie. In truth, I'd grown up in a place as carefully groomed to look pretty as I had been—but it was a festering pit of deceit, manipulation and despair. Studded with jewels, padded with silk-covered pillows, and liberally dusted with a colorful candy shell, my home had been a glorified cage. Not a day has passed that I haven't offered up gratitude for my escape: to the goddess Danu for guiding my steps, to the warrior priestess Kaja who taught me how to survive, and to my brother Harlan who gave up everything to set me free.

Not a day has passed that I didn't recognize that I owed my sanity, likely my very life, to the fact that I escaped Dasnaria. I never wanted to go back.

And yet, here I was: returning to the corrupt and oppressive land of my birth.

I released a sigh into the warm, morning air, and finished the final genuflection in honor of the goddess Glorianna as her sun rose behind me. I stood on a rock promontory, with the sea surrounding me on three sides. With the growing light, the crystalline water brightened to an unearthly shade of turquoise I'd never imagined could be real. I loved my home in Nyambura with my wonderful husband Ochieng, and my four brilliant—if occasionally trying—children, but the beauty of Annfwn took my breath away.

Annfwn was an actual paradise. And not only because of the tropical lushness. The Tala who made the dazzling cliff city their home possessed a natural free-spiritedness that made for a relaxed and joyful community. Maybe being shapeshifters made them more mentally and emotionally flexible. Regardless, they didn't seem to be bound up in oppressing anyone or trying to exploit each other for power.

Not like in Dasnaria.

Rising to a standing position again, I sent a prayer of gratitude to Glorianna, honoring her as Danu's sister—and in gratitude for the sun that rose every day on my life since I escaped.

"Aren't you supposed to face Glorianna's sun for that?"

The unexpected voice startled me and had me spinning, a dagger in each hand and body coiled into a defensive crouch. Just as quickly, I rose again and sheathed my blades, abashed to realize I'd drawn on Her Majesty Queen Ursula. Who also happened to be Harlan's wife—and was apparently soft-footed enough to sneak up on me. "My apologies, Your Majesty, I—"

"Was rudely interrupted at your prayers."

"Not prayers so much as…" I lifted a shoulder and let it fall, rather than try to explain something so intimate, especially to this woman I barely knew. "I tend to wake early and I enjoy the sunrise." I'd developed the personal celebration long ago, when I'd been an ignorant girl so dazzled by the sun she'd never seen before. All these years later, I still hadn't lost the sense of wonder at its reappearance every morning. "I also wanted to look at the sea. I do know I'm supposed to be facing the sun."

"I doubt that Glorianna cares, and Ami—who might take it

upon herself to instruct you in the proper worship of the goddess—is still lazily abed." Her stern, thin-lipped mouth softened with affection as she referenced Queen Amelia of Avonlidgh.

I supposed, among queens, one's baby sister was still always that. Ursula and I weren't so different that way. I'd never forgotten my younger sisters, Inga and Helva—and only for them would I return to the hellscape that birthed me.

That and vengeance. Though after twenty years, it felt cold, indeed.

"This is a good vantage point," Ursula said, gesturing to the vista and sounding like she was trying to think of things to say to me. Was she feeling awkward also? I had failed to reply to her previous remark, a habit of mine from when I'd taken a vow of silence. If I didn't have anything specific to say, I tended to fall silent.

"Andi comes here all the time," Ursula continued. "It's her special place."

Well, shit. This was Queen of Annfwn's special place. Another younger sister of Ursula, Queen Andromeda was also a terrifyingly powerful sorceress. That made several missteps I'd made so far today and I hadn't been awake all that long.

"I apologize," I said, gauging the space between Ursula and the worn stone lionhead that stood proudly at the end of the rock promontory. I'd walked out along the breakwater initially to get a better look at it. The statue was very like the lions of Nyambura—which were not creatures of this land at all—so I'd been bemused to see it there. Now I was trapped. I couldn't leave without shouldering past the queen, and she didn't look inclined to end the interview yet. "Perhaps we should vacate this spot," I offered tentatively, but Ursula waved that off.

"Andi is not a morning person either," she told me. "She'll

be huddled over a pot of tea for a while yet. Besides, you're our heart-sister, so she'd be fine with you being here."

I didn't know what to say to that. When Ochieng and I had agreed to follow the wandering priestess Kaedrin to this place, she'd told us that Harlan needed my help. Beyond the fact that I owed my brother a debt I could never repay, I'd been entirely caught up with the longing to see him again. It had never once occurred to me that he'd have married—and that his wife would have sisters, who also had husbands, all apparently intent on being my family, too.

I'd grown accustomed to knowing pretty much everyone in our fairly small community of Nyambura. Gaining so many new relatives in one swoop was a bit overwhelming.

Ursula raised a brow at my silence, then nodded at the daggers I'd sheathed. "That double-blade technique looked like a move from one of Danu's martial forms."

I started to shake my head, then nodded. Ursula's brow climbed higher in question and I had to restrain the urge to bow to her. It had been a very long time since I'd been around royalty—Nyambura didn't have much in the way of government, much less hereditary monarchies—and it seemed my long-forgotten habits all wanted to rush up and take over.

This did not bode well for facing Hestar, my horrible eldest brother, now Emperor of Dasnaria, and my even more awful mother, dowager Empress Hulda. They'd expect me to prostrate myself for them and I would not do that ever again. I'd better flense myself of the impulse to bow and scrape to royalty right now.

I straightened my spine and met Ursula's eyes. They were sharp, clear gray, like the edge of the sword she wore at her hip. She had a tough, rangy body and boyish figure—and made no attempt to soften her appearance with her clothing. Instead she wore a curious outfit in shades of silver, with close-fitting pants hugging her long legs, high knee boots, and a sort of long, flowing coat over an embroidered bodice. She wore some simple jewelry—a pendant necklace and stud earrings—and I hadn't forgotten my old life so much that I didn't recognize the quality of the rubies. With perfect clarity and stunning depth of color, the jewels had to be priceless.

The rubies had been cut simply, so they didn't overpower Ursula, too. She had good bones, but her jaw was too strong for beauty and her nose looked like it had been broken at least once. With her pale, lightly freckled skin and short, dark red hair, she was striking, though my mother would have called her hopelessly unattractive.

Funny how clearly I still heard Hulda's voice, more than two decades after she sentenced me to death by marriage.

Ursula returned my scrutiny, clearly waiting out my silence this time. Probably she found me as odd as I did her. I wasn't sure of the reason for this little conversation, but I supposed I should try to make friends with her. If someone like her even had friends.

"It's an adaptation of Danu's forms, yes, though probably not close to the core teaching," I explained. In lieu of bowing, I offered Ursula's one of my daggers hilt first. A kind of peace offering. "My blades were gifted to me by a priestess of Danu. She also taught me basic self-defense by adapting a Dasnarian dance I knew well—the ducerse—for use with the daggers. She didn't have a lot of time to teach me, and though I've kept up the training all this time, I know my technique has... drifted." A nice way of saying I'd pretty much created my own bastardized style, keeping the parts that worked for me and discarding the ones I didn't like.

Ursula examined the blade with interest. "You've cared for

this well. This design is over thirty years old." She handed it back to me with almost ritual formality.

"That's probably about right. I think Kaja had them for some time before she gave them to me."

Ursula's attention intensified almost palpably, enough so that I had to disguise my reflexive adjustment of my grip on the dagger, ready to defend myself. She noted it with the keenness of a warrior at the top of her game, and I recalled Harlan telling me his Essla was the fastest fighter he'd ever seen. Tempted to ease out of her reach, I made myself stand my ground.

"Kaja?" she repeated, an odd quality to her voice. In a less cold and remote woman, I'd have called it emotion.

"She was a priestess of Danu," I started to explain, then I belatedly remembered that Ursula would've known that. In navigating this conversational dance with the High Queen of the Twelve Kingdoms, I'd forgotten that she'd once been the adolescent princess Kaja had gone to Ordnung to train. And that Kaja had died trying to rescue Ursula's mother. The grief surprised me, rising up thick and fast—and, more astonishing, tears glimmered in the warrior woman's eyes, also, softening them to a silvery shimmer like the silks she wore.

"Kaja was a noble warrior and priestess of Danu," Ursula said slowly. She gave me a little smile. "You loved her."

"I did," I admitted. "She saved my life as much as Harlan did. I've missed her every day."

"She is your aunt, you know, if posthumously," Ursula informed me, keen gaze revealing that she knew full well this would be a surprise to me. "Her daughter Jepp married your brother Kral."

I struggled to assimilate that. "Kaja had a daughter, I know, but her name was Jesperanda, and…" Oh.

"Jepp finds 'Jesperanda' a bit cumbersome for every day

use," Ursula confided drily. "She's a warrior, like her mother, and was one of my best scouts until your brother stole her from me."

"So Kral married her?" I responded, sounding faint. The Kral I remembered would never have married such a woman. Of course, I hadn't imagined Harlan would marry someone like Ursula either.

Ursula tilted a hand from side to side, indicating the imprecise nature of the relationship. "Jepp isn't the marrying type, but they are monogamous, which Jepp will no doubt complain about frequently when you meet her."

When I met Kaja's daughter. Yet another heart-sister and with this unexpected connection. We planned to travel to join Kral aboard his ship, the *Hákyrling,* and I'd been so busy wrestling with the tangled nest of old emotions around Kral that I hadn't given any thought to the wife of his they'd mentioned.

Of course, we'd arrived in the midst of a pitched battle. In the aftermath of that, taking care of the wounded and settling all of my people—including my large elephant family—in a place already overstuffed with Tala packed in for a siege, there just hadn't been much time to sort anything.

"I look forward to meeting her," I said, too formally and rather vaguely.

But Ursula cracked a smile, a real one, and I caught a glimpse of the warmth inside her regal shell, like a ray of the sun that dazzled me so. At that moment, I caught a glimpse of why Harlan loved her. Like Ochieng was my sun, perhaps this tough warrior woman had shone light into the shadows of Harlan's dour Dasnarian fatalism. "When do you plan to leave?" she asked me.

"Ah…" I wasn't sure how to reply. "I believe we are at Your Majesty's disposal. Or at Zynda's." The Tala shapeshifter had offered to turn into a dragon and fly us to the *Hákyrling*, which…

"It's a lot to assimilate, I'm sure," Ursula replied, as if reading my mind. "And though generous, I'm not sure Zynda's offer makes the most sense. That's part of what I wanted to ask you—and your people. We could have a strategy session to make plans, but I don't want to step on your toes."

"My… toes?" I echoed, sounding like an idiot. Their Common Tongue was the second language I'd learned—after I discovered the greater world didn't speak Dasnarian—and I hadn't spoken it long before I'd begun to learn the Nyamburan tongue. Ochieng was fluent in both, plus several other languages, and had taught our children, but I tended to be obstinate about practicing. The metaphors, in particular, evaded me.

"The boundaries of your responsibilities, Imperial Princess Jenna," Ursula said, pointedly using my old name and title.

"Jenna died long ago," I replied. "I am Ivariel now."

"That's not who you'll be when you return to the Imperial Palace," Ursula replied, rather ruthlessly cutting through the polite niceties.

She was correct, of course, but it didn't make it any easier to contemplate.

"This will be a difficult mission for you," Ursula continued, watching me keenly, "on a number of levels. I think Ochieng, your children, and your niece, won't understand just how painful this might be."

I lifted my chin. "Do you doubt my ability to stand up to my former family?"

"Not at all," she answered immediately, surprising me. She inclined her head in acknowledgment. "You have an admirable strength of character. I expected that, from what Harlan told me of you, but you're even more than I imagined."

Harlan had told her about me. From the stark look on her face, he'd told her everything—all the terrible, shameful things that happened back then. I should've expected that, but I'd gone so long among people who knew almost nothing of poor Jenna and what had happened to her that I'd grown accustomed to that being secret. Only Ochieng knew it all.

And Harlan. And now Harlan's wife.

~ 2 ~

"**Y**OU DON'T KNOW me," I spat, and though suitably defiant, my voice came out ragged. Not cool, contained Ivariel, but stupid, pitiful, wounded Jenna. Exposed and humiliated—and in front of this tough, composed woman I'd wanted to think well of me—I felt tears perilously close to the surface. I hadn't felt this way for what seemed like a lifetime, and I hated it.

Ursula held up her hands as if pacifying an attacker, and I realized I'd drawn my daggers again. I might as well have reverted to that panicked young girl Kaja had found aboard the *Valeria*. I could almost hear her snorting in derision at my loss of control. At least Kaja's voice in my head was a welcome one. Pulling my poise around me like a shield, I sheathed the daggers again.

"I apologize," Ursula said, sounding truly chagrined. "I bungled that badly."

"No," I replied as coolly as I could under the circumstances. "I should have realized Harlan would have told you all about…" My voice cracked, Danu take me. "Me," I finished lamely.

Ursula lowered her hands, dropping one to the hilt of her sword, not to draw, but to rub a thumb over the cabochon ruby there, as if to soothe herself. "He hasn't," she said, very seriously. "He told me, no one else, and he only spoke of it to me because *he* needed to talk about it." She blew out a breath and looked up at the sky briefly, maybe asking Danu for patience. "That's not entirely true. I do believe it was good for him to talk about it, but he only told me because I forced him into it."

"*Forced?*" I doubted she could've said anything to surprise—or anger—me more. "What did you do to him?"

Unexpectedly, she grinned. "You sound so fierce and ready to protect him. That's good," she added hastily. "I love him, too, so I can appreciate that. What happened was that I found out about your existence from Jepp—who learned it from your sisters Inga and Helva when she was in the Imperial Palace—and I was angry with him. Harlan had never so much as mentioned he had sisters."

"Oh," I said, for lack of anything else. Kaja's daughter had gone to the Imperial Palace? And had met with my sisters. So much I wanted to ask.

"That he'd kept secrets from me was upsetting to me both because I'd thought we had no secrets between us and because those secrets had to do with Dasnaria, an aggressive empire poised to swallow my smaller realm. I was…" She raked a hand through her hair, disordering the untidy tufts already curling in the sea air. "I was also jealous," she admitted, "and worried that he placed his loyalty to you above his love for me."

I gazed back at her in some astonishment, my own pain temporarily numbed by this confession. Where I came from, no woman would admit to such things to someone she barely knew—certainly not to someone she'd just as easily confessed to seeing as a rival in power.

"No one else knows," she repeated. "Except for Jepp, and she knows only the outlines. As far as everyone else is concerned, you're Harlan's long-lost sister who fled Dasnaria for obvious reasons."

Much more composed now, I raised a brow at that.

"Because Dasnaria pretty much sucks for women," she explained, "so far as any of us can tell. I'm amazed there hasn't been a mass exodus."

I surprised myself yet again by laughing—and she smiled crookedly, and with relief. "They might if we equipped them with enough shoes and taught them to manage money on their own."

"That would be a good start," she agreed gravely. Behind her, I spotted Ochieng and the children—all right, yes, they were all adults by Nyamburan measures except for my youngest, Helvalesa, but they were all still children to me—bringing the elephants down to the water. Ursula followed my gaze, turning to watch the spectacle as the elephants waded into the surf with enthusiasm. Efe, one of the smallest but with an outsized heart, scampered in at top speed.

"It's salt water," Ursula cautioned as Efe plunged her trunk into the water.

"They're not stupid," I retorted. And then Efe stuck her trunk in her mouth, drank—and spectacularly spit it out again from both mouth and trunk. I groaned. "Or maybe they are."

Ursula burst out laughing, a loud and hearty sound, and one that made her face come alight with such personality that I mentally corrected all of my uncharitable thoughts about her lack of beauty. It reminded me of Ochieng's laugh, which now echoed over the water as he waded out to soothe Efe's wounded pride. Violet, matriarch of the herd, complacently sucked up sea water and showered herself with it, very clearly showing Efe how wise elephants handled the ocean. Ochieng spotted us and waved—then went under when a petulant Efe took advantage of his distraction to dunk him.

Ursula turned sparkling eyes on me. "They're extraordinary. The elephants, I mean. Though your family is, too."

"They are," I agreed, pride welling up in me as my family—human and elephant—engaged in a game of dunking and dodging. Then I leveled a serious look on this new heart-sister of mine. "You owe me nothing, but I would appreciate it if... you would keep my secrets. Ochieng knows, but the children don't."

She considered me, all humor fleeing her face, fully the monarch again. "I have three things to say to that. First of all, your secrets, and Harlan's, are not mine to share. Second, I do owe you a great deal since your timely arrival made all the difference between us winning the battle against Deyrr. Finally, I wouldn't betray my worst enemy on such a thing." Her eyes went opaque and she gazed off into some middle distance. "You and I share another sort of sisterhood—one far more painful."

I caught my breath, beyond surprised now. I couldn't imagine her as the helpless prey that innocent Jenna had been. Besides, once I'd fled Dasnaria, I hadn't met another woman who'd suffered what I had. Back in the seraglio, sexual encounters regularly caused wounds—physical and otherwise—but in Nyambura, such things were virtually unheard of. The extended family groups taught their boys better, and dealt sternly with offenders. No family would tolerate the shame of having a predator like my late ex-husband in their midst.

I'd forgotten that other parts of the world weren't like that, and that what I'd gone through wasn't limited to a Dasnarian seraglio.

Ursula seemed to take my stunned silence for offense, because she added, "I don't mean to compare myself. What happened to me was nothing compared to what you went through."

"I'm not sure these things have relative scales of measurement," I said slowly. "I'm sorry for your pain." It was a translation of a Nyamburan phrase that conveyed much more in that tongue, but she took it the right way.

"I appreciate that and return the sentiment." She cast her gaze down, toeing a rock with her boot. "This is not ... something I normally discuss. As in, I don't talk about it with people, ever. If I can help it."

"I'm quite surprised you are," I admitted, recovering my wits enough to realize that a queen like this wouldn't have made a special point to talk with me alone just to chat about our feelings. I suspected we were getting to the crux of why she'd cornered me.

"Yes, well." She winced. "You can blame Harlan for the fact that I speak of it at all."

I grimaced in sympathy. "Ochieng is much the same."

She tilted her head with a wry nod. "The only reason I'm putting us both through this very uncomfortable conversation is I realize going back there will be difficult for you. It will take a great deal of courage."

"I'm not afraid," I replied, though not as sharply as I might have, given what else she'd confessed to me.

"That's good," she replied wryly, "because *I* would be, in your place."

I sagged a little, inside the shell of my bravado. "Ochieng is worried," I told her, and she nodded with perfect understanding. Oddly, as different as I'd thought Ursula and I were, she might understand better than anyone.

"Harlan is worried, too, though he won't say so." She paused, considering. "That's why I wanted to speak to you privately. I think you should take Harlan with you."

I pretended to watch the elephants while I collected my thoughts. She and Harlan had already discussed, not just in my hearing, but in front of everyone, that they'd be returning to the seat of the High Throne at Ordnung. "But you would not being going to Dasnaria with us."

"No." She sounded drily amused. "I have responsibilities here, and as much as it would be interesting to adventure to Harlan's homeland, my visit would be tantamount to a foreign invasion."

She had a point. Still. "It wouldn't be any easier for Harlan to return to that place, to our former family."

"True, and I'm glad you recognize that. To be perfectly honest, I don't want him to go."

I transferred my attention back to her face. "He already declared his place is with you. Even if he hadn't, the *Elskathorrl* demands it. You have that vow and, as his wife, you *do* own his primary loyalty—far more than a nearly forgotten sister."

She shook her head sharply. "Harlan never forgot you. He'll go if you ask him to, if you tell him you need him with you."

"You *want* me to test if his loyalty to me outweighs his to you?"

"Not at all. He'd choose me, for all the reasons you cite. But if you convince him of your need, then I can be the better person and agree." She cracked a thin and cagey smile.

I found myself stroking the scars on my wrist, the ridges a permanent reminder of my late ex-husband and all the scars he put on me, outside and in. "I don't know that I need him with me."

"Maybe not." She inclined her head, acknowledging that. "But I do know that it will tear him apart to worry about you going on your own. Even if you think you don't need him, *he* needs to go, for his own sake as well as yours."

I considered her with new respect—and a growing appreciation. She seemed like a hard woman, sharp-edged as her sword, but she clearly loved Harlan with the selflessness he deserved. "I'll consider your words," I said.

She dipped a nod. "That's all I ask. Well, not all," she amended. "I'd prefer if you didn't tell him I asked this of you, for obvious reasons."

I grinned, understanding her perfectly. "Is he still that obstinate?"

Groaning, she rolled her eyes. "I don't know what he was like then, but I'm going to say he's only gotten worse."

"He was a fourteen-year-old boy who defied our family of tyrannical monsters and the customs of an empire to set me free," I said simply. "Once Harlan sets his mind to something, he never wavers."

"Don't I know it," she muttered, making me wonder exactly how their unconventional relationship had come to be.

"Speaking of," I nodded to the beach over her shoulder, "here he comes now."

She turned, standing beside me, and we both watched as Harlan picked his way along the uneven and rocky path along the top of the breakwater. He'd grown so much bigger over the years. Of course he had, since he'd been an adolescent then and fully a man now. But he'd also broadened more than I expected. Since our parting—and since our family stripped him of his rank as Imperial Prince of Dasnaria, disowned and exiled him—he'd been making his living in the world as a mercenary. His physique showed it, with an exceptionally large and sculpted muscular chest, arms and shoulders. His massive thighs carried his bulk easily and he moved with light grace. With some surprise, I recognized my own dancer's lithe skills in him.

"You look alike," Ursula murmured, watching also. "Which sounds odd, since you're obviously very different, but..."

"But we look alike," I agreed. I'd gained muscle, too, over

the years of training in Danu's arts, dancing, and sometimes defending our home from aggressors. Working with the elephants required strength, if you didn't want to spend half your day knocked on your ass. Still, I'd always remained slender, especially compared to the Nyamburan women, who tended to be more solidly built. So some of that feeling of being slight came from comparison to them, but even Helvalesa, who was no older than my baby sister Helva when I left Dasnaria, already outweighed me.

I'd grown so used to being among Ochieng's people that I'd forgotten what it was like to see my own features on someone else. Harlan and I shared the same wide cheekbones, the high Konyngrr forehead, and our smiles were the same. We shared the taciturn Dasnarian tendency to look grim at rest, so we grimaced more than smiled. Or maybe that was our shitty upbringing.

"You were gone when I awoke," Harlan called out as he drew near.

"He hates that I can slip out without waking him," Ursula confided quietly, then raised her voice. "You were sleeping so soundly, and I knew you needed the rest. How's the injury?"

He rotated the arm on the side that had been wounded in the battle, demonstrating the ease of movement. "Nothing like Tala healing. Good morning, Jen—Ivariel, I mean." He grimaced ruefully. "I'm still getting used to that."

"It's all right," I told him.

He shook his head like a dog shaking off water. "No, it's not. You changed your name for a reason and I need to respect that."

"Well, at first I changed it so they couldn't find me," I explained, to both of them, as Ursula seemed to be listening with interest. "Then…" How to explain? "Ivariel was everything Jenna wasn't. It was easier to embrace the new me than fix the old one."

Harlan looked angry. "There was nothing about you that needed fixing."

"No, I know. I meant that…" I lifted a shoulder and let it fall. "It's difficult to explain and something I'd prefer not to dwell on."

"Of course." He nodded, then looked between us. "What were you two talking about?"

"Did you think I'd eat your sister for breakfast?" Ursula asked mildly, but with a steel edge beneath it.

He considered her, then grinned. "No, but only because Ivariel is as good with a blade as you are."

She snorted inelegantly, nothing regal in it. "You joke, but she just might be. I'll leave you two to talk."

"You don't want to spar?" he asked, cocking his head and reading her intently.

Laying a hand on his cheek, she softened, smiling at him. "Spend some time with your sister. I'm fine. And I have things to do."

"A raft of messages arrived for you," he admitted.

She sighed in resignation. "Of course they did. I'll see you later." With that she strode off, silvery coat streaming like a banner around her long form.

~ 3 ~

"**W**HAT DO YOU think of her?" Harlan asked me, sounding a bit shy, even tentative.

"I think you wouldn't have pledged *Elskathorrl* to someone unworthy of you," I replied.

He narrowed his eyes at me. They'd darkened over the years, the boyish dove-gray flintier now, just as everything about him had hardened and toughened. It made my heart ache a little for that boy who'd once shone with such enthusiasm for life. He'd always been the softest of us, except for maybe Helva, who was his full sister. Their mother, Jilliya, had possessed a kindness, also—far more so than my own mother—and Jilliya had suffered for it.

So, I shouldn't be sorry that Harlan had grown so flinty over the years. Softness equaled weakness—I'd learned that lesson well—and weakness brought only pain.

"That was a graceful non-answer," Harlan commented. "Have you learned diplomatic dancing over the years?"

"I learned those skills at my mother's knee," I replied gently. "It's just that, during the time we spent together, I had no ability to wield those weapons." The stark memory of those days rushed back as if it had been only weeks ago. The terrible pain I'd been in from where my late ex-husband had ripped into me. That excruciatingly cold flight through the mountains, the bitter fear of discovery a metallic taste in my mouth.

From the haunted cast to Harlan's face, he was recalling the same events, and I regretted my words. "I do like Ursula," I said, realizing as I spoke the words that I meant them. "She is somewhat prickly, and not at all elegant or refined—not the kind of woman I would have expected you to marry—but I can see why she appeals to you."

"If I'd stuck to expectations, I'd have been married advantageously to some girl who'd been raised to be little more than a slave groomed to please me," Harlan bit out.

His vehemence took me aback—definitely not the gentle boy I'd known—but I also understood what had driven him. "And Ursula is nothing like that."

He opened his mouth, then closed it and smiled with some chagrin. "My Essla is nothing like that," he agreed. "The first time I saw her, she wore filthy fighting leathers and was covered in road dust. She stalked into King Uorsin's court—and you have to understand everyone was terrified of him—and proceeded to outwit him like her tongue was a sword."

"And you fell in love," I supplied, smiling at the image. I could just picture it.

"I did," he agreed. "Within minutes. Though I had to wear down Essla's formidable defenses. She was no easy conquest."

"Thus the perfect woman for you," I replied, enjoying how he lit up speaking of her.

"True," he admitted. "And you, with Ochieng?"

I felt my lips curving in a soft smile, my gaze going to where Ochieng clung to Violet's back, coaching her in a water battle with Bimur, ridden by Ayela, who seemed to be winning. "With Ochieng it took a very long time," I said. "He conducted a campaign of such subtle wooing that I didn't realize what he was about until I found my heart entwined with his."

"I'd like to get to know him," Harlan said.

"To know Ochieng is to get to know the elephants," I told him.

"I'd like to do that, too." He grinned, then sobered. "I'm so happy you found the elephants."

For the second time that morning, tears pricked my eyes. "I wish you had been with me. I thought of you every day. We should've had the elephants together."

He wiped his own tears away, unembarrassed by his emotions. "We have them now. I'd love to get to know your elephants, too."

"Come on then." I held out my hand, and he took it. Something inside me—a piece that had felt broken for so long I'd forgotten to notice it anymore—shifted and settled again into place.

TRUE TO HER word—really, I should've expected nothing less—Ursula called a strategy meeting that afternoon. Oh, she pretended to defer to the local king and queen, Rayfe and Andromeda, but it was clear to me that no one forgot she was the High Queen and still in charge of the strategy.

We'd all cleaned up from frolicking in the surf, then Harlan had eaten lunch with me, Ochieng and the children. They'd all been very interested to get to know their famous uncle. His namesake and our only son, Shaharlan, had been in raptures. I'd finally shooed them off and now Ochieng, Harlan and I entered the large council chamber carved into the cliff side, truly a marvel of engineering. Or of magic. Difficult to say with these Tala. Spotting Ursula bending over some charts, deep in conversation with a stern-looking soldier type, Harlan went immediately to her.

"Are you doing all right, my love?" Ochieng asked in the Nyamburan dialect, sliding an arm around my waist.

I leaned into him, his warm, strong body so familiar to me after so many years of sharing his bed. He'd braced me through all four of our children's births, and through emotional trials as well, unfailingly and generously giving me all of his heart. I was beyond grateful to have him with me on this new journey. Ursula's words still chased each other around my head. She was right that I hadn't really thought about what it would mean to return to the Imperial Palace, to face the place of my nightmares.

To confront my mother again.

"Yes," I replied in the same language. "It's just a lot, you know?"

"I do know." He waved a hand at the gathering, an odd assortment of the wild-looking, long-haired Tala. A man covered in scaled tattoos like a dragon, and who was king of some nearby islands also loomed. "There is so much new and startling here," Ochieng continued, "that I feel as if I must have fallen asleep and be dreaming one of my own tales." He smiled softly at me, concern in his eyes. "As unsettled as I am, I know it's nothing to what you must be feeling."

"Excuse me," said a petite woman holding a newborn. She was the wife of the dragon-tattooed king—I'd forgotten her name already—and though she lacked the markings, she was as deeply tanned as he. With her small stature, bronze-flecked brown eyes and sun-streaked brown hair, she reminded me of the *nyrri*, the wood sprites of Dasnarian tales. "I know it's beyond rude of me to interrupt," she continued, "but I'm so curious about the language you're speaking. Is that the language of Chiyajua?"

"You are not rude at all, Queen Dafne Nakoa KauPo," Ochieng replied in Common Tongue, bowing. Of course Ochieng would remember her name and title. "Chiyajua is a large continent and has never been united as your Thirteen Kingdoms were with a single trade tongue, so there is no language that can be pointed to as Chiyajuan. Ivariel and I were speaking the dialect peculiar to our village of Nyambura, and the surrounding region."

Her eyes sparked with interest. "It sounds like a pitched language, but with glottals similar to the dialects of our southern kingdoms, such as Elcinea and Nemeth."

"Indeed!" Ochieng smiled broadly. "The languages must have a common root because I readily learned some of the Elcinea tongues when I first traveled to the Port of Ehas as a young man."

"Is that where you acquired Common Tongue?" she asked. "Your command of it is flawless."

"You flatter me. I only wish it to be flawless, but I do practice assiduously. As Ivariel and I have been raising our family, I have traveled less—staying close to home where I'm needed—and few there care to converse with me. I mostly expand my knowledge of the language by reading. I have a most interesting book of tales from the Isles of Remus that includes many words I don't know. Perhaps you could translate them for me?"

"I'd be happy to as I'd love to see that book. The Remus Isles have incorporated some of the language of Kooncelund, so they may not be Common Tongue words at all."

"I have the book with me, do you think I have time to fetch it before the meeting begins?"

"You've lost him now," said a voice in my ear.

I turned to find Queen Andromeda standing beside me. She rested her hands on her very pregnant belly, wry amusement in her storm gray eyes. I'd describe her as a softer version of Ursula—not so sharp and steely, her long hair much darker with only hints of red—but magic seemed to rise from her like the thick mist billowing off the river in the mornings back home.

"Is the losing of husbands to conversations about books and language a common occurrence here?" I asked.

"Yes, if Dafne is involved," she replied very seriously, but with a twinkle lightening her eyes with crystal flecks.

"I'll be on guard," I replied in the same tone. "I appreciate the warning, Queen Andromeda."

"Please." She wrinkled her nose. "Everyone calls me Andi."

"Except for me, my Andromeda." King Rayfe appeared at her side like a predator sliding out of ambush. Where his wife's hair was the sort of black that verges into bloodred, his went towards blue. Glossy as an obsidian dagger, falling long and straight, it reminded me of a mane as much as anything. His eyes were deeply and radiantly blue, striking in an already charismatic face. I'd have known him for a wolf anywhere. "Have your people received appropriate accommodations and the provisions they need, Ivariel?" he inquired with smooth charm.

"Yes, thank you very much. I know you didn't expect several dozen elephants to be dumped in your laps—and they require a great deal of food."

"The Tala love animals," he replied easily, running a hand over Andi's hair and smiling at her with affection. "We are delighted to learn more about your elephants. Some of our people are able to take that form, but it's unusual enough that the animal is nearly as mythical to us as Zyr's gríobhth form."

My gaze slid of its own accord to the wild-looking Tala man leaning against the wall on the far side of the room, talking with Kral's former wife, Karyn. He was intent on her—seeming as if he was trying to convince her of something, in fact—but her gaze was on me. Oh, she averted her eyes immediately, demurely lowering them in fine female Dasnarian fashion. Very little else about her demeanor spoke of Dasnarian feminine meekness, however. She carried a quiver and an unstrung bow—and carried herself with a kind of confident determination no chit married off to, then divorced by Kral should've been able to muster. She'd told me I'd been an inspiration to her, which seemed beyond unlikely. The Tala man—Zyr, apparently—tugged on her hair and though she blushed, her gaze that flashed up to his held fire. Interesting.

"A gríobhth form?" I asked.

"You might know it as a gryphon," Ochieng supplied, rejoining me.

"Do you know *everything*?" I asked in exasperation.

"Yes," he replied, as if surprised I'd even asked. "You've been married to me this long and you still haven't realized that?"

I shook my head and raised a brow. "Already weary of your new love?"

"Not at all. We've planned a tryst for later when we'll snuggle up with some books." He waggled his own brows at me.

"You might be wary of yon dragon king," I advised, casting a wary glance at the stern and towering man.

"La! *I* have an army of elephants. He doesn't frighten me." Ochieng grinned broadly.

"King Nakoa KauPo can summon storms," Andi confided.

"Truly?" Ochieng regarded the dragon king with newfound respect. "Handy skill. I wonder if he could do the reverse—we have a rainy season that could stand with shortening."

I elbowed him. "Don't be mucking with the balance of nature."

He gave me a wounded look. "I said shortening, not banishing."

Rayfe laughed, taking Andi's hand. "See? Other married couples bicker, too."

She rolled her eyes. "Don't start with me. And they've been together long enough to have adult children. We've barely started." She ran a hand over her swollen belly and I followed the gesture with a practiced eye.

"Another few weeks to go?" I asked.

"It looks that way," she agreed, and I recalled that Andi also had the gift of foresight. She likely knew exactly when the baby would come. "Don't tense," she said to Rayfe, squeezing his hand.

He grimaced, gaze going to her belly. "I'm working on it." But he didn't look happy.

Ochieng clapped him on the shoulder. "It doesn't get easier, standing by while the woman you love labors so hard, but remember that she depends on you to care for her. This is a very important job, that one no one else can do, because no one else knows her as well as you do."

Rayfe met Andi's gaze. "Think that's true?"

"I know it is," she replied, and they fell silent, eyes intent on the other, making me wonder if they could speak to each other without audible words.

"All right, people," Ursula called, straightening her sheaf of papers. "Let's have a conversation about dealing with this enormous, unstoppable navy *still* heading our way. Ivariel, this is your party now. What's your plan?"

~ 4 ~

I'D COME A long way from the broken girl I'd been, and though I'd taken on various leadership roles in the D'Tiembo family, both domestic and martial, I'd also worked hard to shed the imperious arrogance drilled into me through the focused efforts of my ambitious mother. Losing that attitude had been partly to hide my identity—*No princess!* Kaja's ghost reminded me—but I'd also been more than relieved to rid myself of the shallow and vain Imperial Princess Jenna.

In many ways, she represented the worst of Dasnaria. Had my first marriage been less brutal, I might now be exactly like my mother. I might've conspired with her to resurrect the cult of Deyrr and the evil High Priestess. I had no gift of foresight, but I could clearly see that other self I could have become. Harlan possessed an inherent goodness I'd lacked. If Jenna hadn't been broken beyond repair, burnt to ash, then resurrected as Ivariel, I might not have had the cruelty and ambition excised from my being.

I knew I still retained much of that imperious tendency to take charge and fling orders about—Ochieng never failed to remind me, and I'd seen my new heart sisters take note of it— and so being truly in charge felt like a dangerous dance taking me too close to the flame that had birthed me.

And yet, I also knew that this war was mine to wage. This

was my unfinished business.

So, though I didn't much care to take charge of this gathering of monarchs and magic workers, all eyes were on me, thanks to Ursula. She was giving me an expectant stare, probably knowing exactly how little I liked this ball she'd lobbed at me. And Ochieng, who did indeed know me better than anyone, poked me in the small of my back with a pointy finger, prodding me forward.

"Let's sit," I said, moving to the chair closest to me. The big table was oval, which made it more egalitarian, but the large chairs at the end farthest from the door clearly belonged to Rayfe and Andi, as the local royalty. Watching the rest of them arrange themselves around the table gave me a few moments to assess the alignments and personalities of the assembly.

"Is there an update on the progress of the ships Hestar has sent against you?" I inquired of Ursula, since she'd been going over the papers.

"I spoke with Jepp a bit ago," Andi answered instead, then smiled at my surprise and tapped her temple. Oh, she meant she'd mentally reached across that distance. Sorcery indeed. "Jepp and Kral say that Nakoa's storm has the navy sailing in circles still, but that it seems to be breaking up."

"I can bend the forces of nature to my will for only so long," the dragon king inserted in a low, rumbling voice.

"We're indebted to you for the breathing room," Ursula told him, and he inclined his head. "How long do we have?"

"A day or two," he said. "I unhappily regret it cannot be more."

"That doesn't give us much time, but I understand." She looked at me. "We have ships sailing to confront Hestar's navy, to supplement the ones there with the *Hákyrling*, but we are gravely outnumbered. If it's at all possible, I'd prefer to avoid a battle entirely."

I had to admire her for that. Battles only got the soldiers killed while the perpetrators stayed home safe and swathed in silks. "We heard from the High Priestess of Deyrr's own mouth that my mother, Dowager Empress Hulda, is behind this attack. Do we believe the emperor is aligned with her?" I asked the latter of Harlan.

He dipped his chin in grim affirmation. "Jepp saw Hestar engaged in… unsavory activities with the High Priestess at the Imperial Palace."

I wasn't at all surprised at Hestar's ambition—or his perversions—but he and Hulda had never been political bedfellows. Quite the opposite, and I said as much.

"We think they began colluding only recently," Harlan supplied. "Since you and Kral were her only children, once Kral defected, Hulda lost her game piece in the conniving for the throne. With Hestar on the throne, it makes sense that she'd have to cozy up to him, especially as everyone assumes you are dead."

"Not *everyone* believes that," Karyn said, then blushed at my raised brow. "I mean, I beg your pardon for correcting you, Consort, but—"

"Can we say that the previous rules abolishing titles and apologies for purposes of streamlining discussion are still in place?" Andi asked with gentle exasperation.

"Of course…" Karyn replied, and I heard the pause where she mentally added the title, but she gamely kept going. "The legend of the lost princess of Dasnaria is pervasive and often repeated, at least among women." She gave me a shy smile. "I grew up on the whispered stories of how you escaped a terrible marriage and went overseas to gather your power and allies. Many believe you will return in triumph some day, like the legendary heroes of old. Only for women."

Beside me, Ochieng wiped a hand over his mouth, clearly restraining a sarcastic comment about my heroic status, and I slid him a narrow glare of warning. "Unfortunately, I am only a mortal woman."

"Your proposed return is rather uncannily close to the legend Karyn describes, however," Ursula pointed out, tapping her callused fingers on the arm of her chair. "You did travel far away, gained new skills, and will be returning with a magical army of allies. You'd be a fool not to take advantage of the potency of that myth come real, and the people's yearning for you to be their savior."

She had a point, though I didn't love the idea. *No princess!* Surely posing as a goddess was even worse. I decided to focus on the details. "Am I returning with an army of magical allies, though?" I asked pointedly. "I have my family and people, including the elephants, but that hardly qualifies."

"The elephants will seem as dazzling mythical beasts to the Dasnarians," Ochieng put in.

"Karyn and I are going with you," Zyr said, holding up their interlaced hands. "We got skunked on the battle, so we want in on this part. And Karyn would like to visit her family."

"Yes," Karyn agreed. "My father will no doubt wish to interrogate my new husband." She added a sweet smile at Zyr's stricken jolt.

"As I offered before," said the dark-haired woman who resembled Zyr, "I'm willing to go, and Marskal with me." She indicated the stern soldier who'd been reporting to Ursula, then pointed to herself. "I'm Zynda," she clarified, "the one who can become a dragon."

"I'd love to see Dasnaria," Dafne said wistfully, "but Nakoa and I should return home, to take care of our own islands and this one." She shifted the sleeping infant in her arms. "But Kiraka—the big gold dragon—is interested to go with you."

My magical army did seem to be growing. "Anyone else?"

"Ash is sleeping off healing the wounded and will be back at it when he wakes," Andi noted, "so Ami is staying here for a while. But Ami wants us to remind anyone who's going that Kir, traitor to the Thirteen Kingdoms and former High Priest of the Church of Glorianna, is hiding out at the Imperial Palace. Or was, the last we knew. She'd like him brought back to face trial for his crimes."

I nodded, making a mental note. "You're not coming?"

"No," she replied. "I need to work with Stella—my niece—and Rayfe would like to teach our nephew Astar about shapeshifting discipline, so we'll also remain here. Besides which, I'm under orders to stay close to home." She laid a hand on her belly and Rayfe put his hand over hers, giving her a grateful smile.

He then turned to me. "That said, any Tala who'd like to travel with you have our permission. Many of our people lost loved ones to Deyrr, and they will appreciate the opportunity to redress those losses." His glittering feral smile made the short hairs on the back of my neck stand up, and I was just as glad not to be facing him in wolf form.

"And Ursula and I must return to Ordnung," Harlan put in. I carefully did not look at Ursula. "But I think Kral will want to go with you."

"Where Kral goes, Jepp goes," Andi added, "so I can communicate with you, should you need reinforcements. Or magical assistance."

"Can you perform sorcery from that far away?" I asked.

She shrugged. "Some."

"By which she means, staggering amounts," Zynda put in

with a sly smile.

"Maybe," Andi cautioned. "I've never tried to reach that far."

Zynda shrugged elaborately. "For that matter, I can do a few minor magics, should we need it."

Interesting. "I don't see us defeating the Dasnarian Empire by force," I noted drily, "so I'm inclined to think a small team would be most effective. We go, maybe rally the populace, if you think that will work," I nodded to Karyn, "then remove Hestar and Hulda from power. Then the navy can be recalled so they no longer threaten these lands. Though, that might take longer than two or three days."

"If it does, it does," Ursula acknowledged.

"Who will you put on the throne?" Harlan inquired. "Will you establish yourself as empress?"

"No!" I burst out, and was sure I heard Ochieng snicker quietly. "That is," I said, gathering my wits, "I am already married, and though I know it's acceptable, I would not marry one of my brothers regardless."

Harlan regarded me somberly. "You still have too much Dasnarian in you." He gestured to Ursula. "You could be empress on your own blood claim to the throne. As our father's firstborn, you have that right."

The possibility struck me with force. And Harlan was correct—I did have enough Dasnarian in me still that it hadn't occurred to me. I also had enough of my mother in me to find the prospect exhilarating. All through my childhood she'd drummed into me that only power mattered. Power protected you and provided everything you could want. As Empress of Dasnaria, I'd arguably be the most powerful person in the entire world. It would be a fine revenge on those who'd thought to make me their pawn. I could make changes to the empire, transform Dasnaria into what it could be.

"This is sounding more like a coup than a conquest," Ochieng said, giving me a considering look. He'd always been able to read me well, knowing my thoughts even when we'd been strangers and I'd been under a vow of silence.

"A coup is probably accurate," I conceded.

"But one founded in righteousness," Karyn supplied. "For the good of the people of Dasnaria."

I hoped so. "We need to strike a decisive blow to remove the diseased head from the neck of the empire before the body is too far gone to be saved. After that, we can discuss governance. Are the rest of our Konyngrr siblings still alive?" I directed this last at Harlan, who was watching me with quiet speculation.

"So far as we know, yes. Inga and Helva remain in the seraglio of the Imperial Palace."

"Are they married?" I asked.

"No," Ursula answered, canting her head at me. "As you negotiated for them."

I was surprised that deal had stuck. At most I'd been hoping to buy my sisters some time, but I'd figured that Hulda would find a way to betray the bargain we'd made. Of course, when I left on my wedding journey, I hadn't expected to be gone for nearly twenty-five years. "And our other brothers?"

Dafne spoke up. "According to our best intelligence, we believe Mykal took over the navy following Kral's exile. Leo and Loke seem to be in charge of other military branches."

"Ban is still the same," Harlan told me. "He hasn't the wit to choose sides, so is likely Hestar's puppet."

I nodded, remembering Ban's childlike mind, even as a boy of sixteen. "You knew our brothers better than I did." I'd known them as children, barely met them again years later when I left the seraglio to be married, and then I was gone again. "Do you think they're loyal to Hestar, or simply obligated?"

Harlan lifted a shoulder and let it fall. "I've been gone nearly as long as you have. Inga and Helva would know."

"And are eager to share information," Ursula added.

"Is there a way to contact my sisters?" I asked.

They exchanged glances. Dafne handed the baby to her husband and checked some notes. "Maybe?" she said doubtfully. "I have a contact there, a librarian from our island named Akamai, but since hostilities escalated, our correspondence has broken off."

"Kral will also be able to discuss our brothers," Harlan said, still watching me.

Kral. Much as I dreaded confronting the brother who'd tried to send me back into that nightmare of a marriage that would've seen me broken and eventually dead, it seemed I needed him. I looked to Zynda. "It seems I should take you up on the offer to visit the *Hákyrling*." I glanced at Ochieng for his confirming nod. "Then we can make our final decisions on this righteous coup."

"We can go now, if you like," Zynda said. She had large eyes in an exotically angled face, and they were a deep blue like Rayfe's and her brother's. At the moment, they sparkled with anticipation. "I'd love to stretch my wings."

"You nearly flew your wings off yesterday," Marskal said to her with narrowed eyes.

"Yes. *Yesterday*. I'm rested now," she replied saucily. "I can carry you, Ochieng, and Ivariel easily."

I glanced at Ochieng, hoping he could read my thoughts now, and would understand. "If Ochieng remained in Annfwn for the moment, could you bring Harlan instead?" I met Harlan's surprised gaze, noted Ursula's quiet attention. "Would you come with me, baby brother?" I heard the earnest plea in my own voice. Yes, I asked in part to lay the groundwork to accommodate my heart-sister's request, but also I'd felt a stirring in my soul I hadn't felt in decades. It had always felt like a snake to me, a serpent of hatred that was broken, enraged Jenna. It hissed and uncoiled in the cold ashes at the bottom of my heart at the thought of Kral and the part he'd played in my marital enslavement. What if I lost control and tried to kill him? Not only would I fail myself, but I'd perhaps murder the beloved of Kaja's daughter. I owed Kaja's memory better than that.

Under the table, Ochieng put a hand on my knee, squeezing firmly—and a piece of my anxiety relaxed. Of course he understood.

Harlan had exchanged a similar silent communication with Ursula and nodded. "If Zynda is amenable to my weight in exchange for Ochieng's…" His eyes lingered on Ochieng, however, and I appreciated his consideration as Zynda breezily agreed.

"Excellent," Ochieng said. "This gives Dafne and me time to discuss a certain book?"

She lit up. "Yes, please. That is, if—"

Nakoa laughed. "I will keep our Lena while you go play with your books."

"I say we're done then," Ursula announced, pressing hands to the table and levering herself to her feet. "You kids go play—and figure out how to stop that fleet where it is—while we do some work. King Rayfe, Queen Andromeda, I have some documents for you to review and—"

"Oh, Moranu, no," Andi exclaimed, turning to Rayfe in appeal. "Save me."

He patted her hand. "Courage, my queen. Documents pertaining to what?"

Ursula smiled thinly. "With the barrier gone, our border agreements are obsolete. We need to revise them."

Rayfe grimaced. "All of them? That's nearly a hundred treaties."

"A hundred and five," Ursula replied with cruel cheer. "So we'd better get started."

Andi groaned. "I'm sending for more tea. And wine."

"Food, too," Rayfe reminded her with a knowing smile.

She smiled back. "That too."

~ 5 ~

O CHIENG AND I walked together down to the beach where we were to meet Zynda, Marskal, and Harlan. He held my hand as we strolled along the walk through the vibrant and bustling cliff city, as if we were tourists come simply to visit a new land. Once I'd become accustomed to thinking of the place as a vertical version of a city, it felt more familiar. The scars of battle lingered, but already people were working to rebuild. Even the children helped to scrub away burn marks from dragon fire, and the elderly and bandaged wounded gathered under bright silk awnings, their hands busy with food, cloth and other items.

"Thank you for understanding," I said to Ochieng, squeezing his hand.

He slid me an amused smile, dark eyes sparkling with laughter. "You don't have to thank me for a freedom that has always belonged to you."

"I know that." He understood, too, that my old habits of thinking lingered, that deeply embedded instructions urged me to ask for my husband's permission, that part of me still remained ridiculously afraid of venturing far from his side. I knew better, in my head—but that dutiful daughter deep inside never seemed to be quite convinced. "I'm not sure, however," he continued, giving my hand a reassuring squeeze, "that I *can* completely understand."

Oh. Oh no. "It's just that Harlan was there, before, when Kral came to—"

"Tst," Ochieng stopped me with an impatient hiss. "More listening, less talking."

"That's something, coming from you," I grumbled, making him laugh.

"All too true," he admitted ruefully. "But you love me even though I tell long stories and cozy up to clever librarians with big... vocabularies."

"All too true," I replied wryly. "All right—I'm listening."

"What you and your brothers went through, this is a thing you all share. The wounds are old, with thick scars layered over, but the poison remains beneath, festering. I think that only someone else who's felt this same poison can know the bitter sting. I can say, 'oh, how terrible it is that you were poisoned,' but that's as much as I can understand."

"You've always understood me better than anyone, except perhaps for the elephants," I replied staunchly.

"Ah, well, the elephants are always an exception. And I'm ever grateful for what we share," he slid me a smile full of warmth and enduring love. "Still, though we have joined our hearts and lives, we are still individuals, and there are things you must do alone. Or with someone else."

"You're a good man, Ochieng."

"I know," he replied with satisfaction, then laughed heartily when I bumped his shoulder.

We walked on in companionable silence, wending our way lower down the cliff face, taking in the tropical splendor and the way animals mixed freely with humans. The D'Tiembo family lived in close proximity with the elephants, the pattern of life there deeply interwoven with the needs of the elephants. But Annfwn took that interweaving to another level, especially when

I considered that many of these 'animals' were shapeshifters.

"I'm not sure I can face Kral," I finally said, aware that Ochieng had remained quiet, waiting for me to say what was on my mind.

"What are you afraid of?" he asked softly.

"Being weak and pitiful, maybe," I admitted with a little laugh.

"You were never that."

"You didn't know me then," I retorted, then continued before he could argue. "And that's not even really it. I don't know if I can forgive him."

"Then don't." He shrugged when I glanced at him in surprise. "It's not a rule. You are not required to forgive those who hurt you."

I considered that rather astonishing idea. It hadn't occurred to me, that I could withhold forgiveness. "Harlan has forgiven him."

"I think Harlan would be the first to say that his journey toward forgiveness was a shorter and less painful one than yours."

"I don't know about that…" Harlan had filled me in on his time since we parted—how Kral went mindless with rage at losing me in Sjør, how our loving family had beaten him, and then my sisters to extract my location from him. Information he'd been unable to give, not even to prevent our innocent sisters from a flogging. We'd both laughed, and then wept over the Dasnarian certainty that I, an ignorant female, could never have eluded capture without help. They'd been so *certain* that Harlan had to know. He'd finally resorted to the Skablykrr, taking an unshakeable vow not to speak of me, simply to get them to stop.

Funny how we'd both ended up with vows of silence.

I realized I'd fallen into thought and hadn't finished what I'd started to say, Ochieng still waiting patiently for my words, as he always had. *Of course* Harlan had forgiven Kral. Harlan was practically a saint. I couldn't imagine him doing anything else. Me, however… My heart was blackened with rage and hatred. The intervening years had done much to heal it, along with Ochieng's love, the love of the extended D'Tiembo family, the unconditional devotion of my children, and of the elephants. But I recognized the stirrings of that serpent deep within, the one that knew only rage and retribution.

Before the last few days, I would've confidently told anyone who asked that I was healed, that I'd left my past behind. Now, the nearer I drew to my past, the more the gilding seemed to be flaking away, as if it had all been a pretty gloss over the rotted core. "Harlan has always been a better person than I am," I said, trying to explain. "The best of all of us, with a truly good heart."

And I… I was like my mother.

Ochieng stopped walking and drew me onto a little balcony, a wide place in the road out of the teeming foot traffic, over-looking the tranquil sea. He took both of my hands in his and gazed at me with solemn intensity. "Ivariel, my love, *you* have a truly good heart. I would not have shared my bed, my own heart, and my life with you if that weren't so."

I began weeping, the tears pouring out as they had back then, when I'd been so broken, the raw parts of me so exposed, that the tears had just poured out like water from a shattered vase. With a murmur of distress, Ochieng pulled me into his arms, holding me against him while I tried to find a way to stop up the holes again. "I don't know what's wrong with me," I said against his strong chest, his muscles lean and tough from working with the great beasts that were his friends.

"You're facing a very difficult thing," he replied.

"But it's been so long."

"I think emotional pain has no time limit. While Ivariel has grown, moved on, and lived a full life, young Jenna has remained where she was when you left her. Ivariel found her footing, but Jenna never faced what drove her from her home and family."

I pulled back just enough to see his face. "I have faced it. Over and over."

"You faced parts of it. The rest you ran away from."

"I had to run," I snapped, suddenly as angry as I'd just been wretched.

"You can be mad," he replied evenly, "and you can take it out on me, since I'm a convenient target, but no one is saying you didn't have to run. I'm just pointing out that you did run, and now you're going back."

"You're right." I sagged in my regret, aware of raging Jenna boiling under my thin veneer of control. "I'm sorry. I'm being awful."

"You are not being awful." He turned me so my back was against his chest, and wrapped one arm around me, gesturing at the busy scene around us. "You are like this city. Triumphant, but dealing with the destruction still. Battered, burned, tending to wounds, this is the aftermath of battle. No matter what the stories imply, victory isn't followed only by feasting and dancing. There is also the hard work of recovering and rebuilding."

I leaned back against him. "You're saying I've been feasting and dancing all these years and now I must take on the delayed work of rebuilding."

A chuckle rumbled through his body and he kissed my temple. "It's not a perfect analogy. Our lives have not been all feasting and dancing. There's been plenty of rain. And floods. And mud."

"The sun can't shine *all* the time, Ochieng," I said drily.

"True enough," he answered cheerfully. "The rainy season inevitably arrives. And sometimes we must confront our treacherous brothers." He kissed my temple again, lingering this time. "But, you don't *have* to do this, Ivariel. We can load up the ships and go home."

I released a breath. All these people, singing as they cleaned up the aftermath of battle, repairing their homes and shops, working together. "I do have to go, because I made a promise to my sisters."

He hummed thoughtfully. "And Kral is part of that."

"Yes," I conceded.

"Continuing to our appointment on the beach then?" he inquired.

"Painful though it may be," I agreed. I took his hand again and we resumed walking. It seemed the dread weighed on me a little less heavily. "Thank you for talking me down."

"Part of my job," he declared breezily. "I get extra husband points for it."

I bumped his shoulder. "You already have thousands more husband points than I have wife points."

"Well, that's just the way of the world," he said, nodding with a sage expression, and making me laugh.

We rounded a corner and entered an arcade of blossoming vines trained over a trellis to make a tunnel of sweet scent and blazing color. "It's amazing that things like this survived the assault," I commented in wonder.

Ochieng squeezed my hand. "Sometimes beautiful things survive to blossom and grow."

I rolled my eyes. "You're going to wear out this analogy."

We emerged from the floral bower and back into sunlight bouncing off the white sand beach. The brightness made me blink—as did the sight of Zynda in dragon form. Though I'd seen the dragons—both the shapeshifted and the permanent variety—during battle, it was something else to take one in during a calm moment of consideration.

"Who would've imagined we'd ever be privileged to see such a creature?" Ochieng breathed, and I nodded, struck speechless by the sight.

She was enormous. Once upon a time, the elephants had looked huge to me, but Zynda was immense enough to hold Violet in the curving talons that tipped prehensile tarsals at the ends of her forelegs. Surely "paws" was the wrong word, even if "hands" seemed wrong also. She shone like a dark sapphire in the sun, her scales glinting with rippling light. With her wings spread, they dwarfed her body, the supple blue membrane nearly translucent.

She had snaked her head around to watch Marskal attach some kind of harness, reminding me very much of the elephants when we tried a new armor arrangement on them.

"I've always known that the elephants have intelligence much like ours," Ochieng said with interest, and a hint of the same reverence I felt, "but seeing human intelligence in animal form like this…"

"Confirms it?" I asked, and he flashed me a rueful grimace.

"I wonder what Violet would be like if she could shapeshift to human form?"

"Very much like Zalaika," I replied wryly, making him laugh. Ochieng's mother and the elephant matriarch did have a great deal in common.

We were crossing the beach, trading theories on the human appearance of our various elephant family members, when an even more astonishing creature plummeted from the sky, landing with a puff of sand near Zynda. This I had not seen before, and I halted, as if understanding what I was seeing taxed my mind so much I couldn't walk at the same time.

Because the golden-haired Karyn rode the monster's back, I knew this must be Zyr in gryphon form—gríobhth form, I reminded myself. And no wonder Rayfe had referred to the gríobhth as mythical. It looked like nothing I'd ever seen before, or even imagined.

His body reminded me of those lions of Nyambura, but in glossy black, with shimmering sapphire highlights. A whip-like tufted tail matched the lion, too, but the taloned paws belonged more to a raptor—and matched the elegant eagle's head, with lethally curved beak and feathered crest. The feathers flowed smoothly into wings, also like a great bird's, all in shining black sapphire.

"Is it odd that brother and sister share similar coloring in animal form?" I wondered, then laughed at myself, that this was the first observation I could articulate.

"They're twins, even," Harlan said, coming up beside us. "Fraternal twins, not identical like Leo and Loke."

Shaken from the spell, we resumed walking. "I wonder what they're like now," I said, "the twins." They'd been so adorable as toddlers, tawny-haired and green-eyed, always into mischief. It was hard to think of them as leading armies. Of dealing death and being cruel to their wives and rekjabrel.

But then years had passed, and we all had changed.

Harlan was shaking his head. "I have no idea, either. You'll have to tell me, when you see them."

~ 6 ~

T HE YEARNING IN Harlan's voice only confirmed what Ursula had said. I supposed I should resign myself to the reality that she knew my brother much better than I did now. She'd been big enough to want to send Harlan with me, so I could be generous enough to accept the gift of his company.

"We're ready when you are," Marskal called to us and, thus prompted, we began walking again.

Karyn inclined her head as we approached, and I read in her body the tension of a suppressed formal curtsy. Sisters under the skin, she and I, both exiles of Dasnaria, women wandering the world without permission from our fathers and brothers. An impossibility nearly as great as her gríobhth lover. Perhaps that's why she'd been drawn to the Tala shapeshifter, finding another odd soul. I'd have liked to ask her about Kral, but there wouldn't be time.

Besides, I'd find out soon enough for myself.

"Can you climb the rope ladder, Ivariel?" Marskal asked, and I measured it with my eye. Much like mounting an elephant, if exponentially taller. "If not," he added, "Zynda can assist."

She nodded her great head, smoke wafting lazily from her nostrils.

"I can do it," I said, eyeing her and wondering what form that assistance might take.

"Excellent. I'll mount first, then you follow, and Harlan last." He climbed the swinging rope with swift agility, Zynda watching his ascent with loving attention.

I turned to Ochieng. "Look, I'm telling you goodbye to your face."

He laughed and embraced me. "An old joke," Ochieng explained over my shoulder to Harlan.

"Though it wasn't funny, in the beginning," I corrected.

"No." He kissed me and let me go. "And you won't be gone for long. I'll see you back here in a few hours."

"True." I gave him one more kiss. "If I fall off, don't you dare laugh at me."

"I would never," he replied with fake solemnity.

"He's lying," I told Harlan. "He laughed at me every time Violet shook me off and dumped me in the lake."

Harlan grinned and shook Ochieng's hand. "I would love to hear some of these stories, when we return. Heart-brother," he added.

Ochieng gripped Harlan's hand in both of his, clearly moved. "Take care of her."

"I will," Harlan promised, "though, as you noted, we'll only be gone a few hours."

I went to the dangling rope, found the foothold, swinging a bit in the open air until I reached her side—and sending a prayer of gratitude to Danu for the strength I'd developed that allowed me to make the climb. I had to take a moment once I reached Zynda's side, just to run a hand over those shining scales. They looked like they'd been carved from sapphire, but they lay soft and supple as snakeskin. Remarkable.

A blast of brick-oven heat chased the air from my lungs, and I jerked, twisting to find Zynda's dragon head unsettlingly close—a giant blue eye examining me. "I'm fine," I told her. "I was just... You're incredibly beautiful, and so extraordinary." A translucent lid wicked up from the bottom of her eye and down again, and she cocked her head, obviously preening.

"She's terribly vain," Marskal called down to me, "so if you start with the compliments, we'll never get out of here."

Zynda lifted her head and bumped him with it—very gently—and he laughed, stroking her soft snout, then kissing her there. "Yes, yes, you are very beautiful. You dazzle me, quicksilver girl."

Back on task, I climbed with more alacrity, feeling much more at home using the rope lattice to scale her side. Marskal gave me a hand when I reached the top, and—having learned not to refuse the offer of help—I took it to steady myself as I swung in behind him. Harlan followed a few moments later, settling in behind me.

"Remember when we rode like this, through the mountains?" Harlan asked, his voice hoarse with emotion.

"Yes." I sometimes dreamed about that, the terrible pain, feeling the blood leaking out of me from between my legs, and the white-blindness of the blizzard. Harlan was so much larger now at my back. And I'd grown too. "You'll be reassured to know I've since learned to ride." I realized he'd spoken in Dasnarian, and I'd replied in the same, the old language surprisingly easy on my tongue again.

Zynda flexed her wings and Marskal patted her shoulder. Down the beach, Zyr galloped with surprising speed, Karyn folded close against his neck like someone racing a horse. His wings opened and he seemed to labor, skimming close over the gentle surf, then gradually gaining altitude. I was watching them so closely that I wasn't prepared when Zynda launched into the air, leaving my stomach behind. A long shout ripped out of me, echoed by Harlan, and he gripped me around the waist. I deeply regretted joking about falling off.

Marskal turned his head. "Zynda says to tell you she would never let you fall," he shouted over the wind of her passage, leaving me to wonder how she knew my thoughts, and how she'd spoken to him.

WE HAD NO opportunity for conversation on the flight. The wind rushed past so fiercely that we could barely hear each other, even shouting. Besides, I was enraptured with the astonishing sensation of flying. We'd quickly left land behind, striking out over open sea, the brilliant turquoise of Annfwn deepening to a cobalt blue.

It reminded me of that first ocean journey, when I'd escaped Sjør aboard the Valeria, sneaking out of my cabin when I thought I'd be undetected, watching the ocean change from the stormy gray of Dasnaria, then morphing through all the colors and moods of the various seas on the way to Ehas. I'd been so alone—for the first time in my life—and the ship and sea had felt like my only friends. Until Kaja found me and handed me the keys to being alive and in the world again.

The skies darkened and the winds grew chillier, the ocean below tossing with the fury of a storm. Despite my leathers, which had felt far too warm for Annfwn's gentle heat, I was grateful of the bulwark of the two men before and behind me. Then we passed into an area of calm, like the tranquil center of the spinning storms that lashed the coast of Chiyajua. It had a magical quality, Danu's high sun shining from clear blue skies, while all around the thunderclouds circled. It was magical, I supposed—and remarkable to think of Dafne's dragon king making this with his mind.

Below us sailed several ships. The largest, unmistakably Dasnarian in design, also looked like so many of the sailing ships that had been docked at Sjør—and like the ships I'd learned to watch for and avoid when I'd been on the run and hiding. Funny, in a way, that I still flinched inside at the sight, even though I went toward this one of my own free will.

Zynda circled, spiraling down through the now warm and still air. As we neared the ship, which surely must be Kral's *Hákyrling*, it became clear that the dragon's great size dwarfed even the stately sailing vessel. "Where will we land?" I called out, the slower glide of descent allowing for conversation again.

Marskal laughed. "No, you will *not* use Kiraka's method!" He twisted to be able to talk to us. "Kiraka once dumped Zynda and me into the ocean to solve that problem. But Zynda will be gentler with us. But be quick, because it's hard work for her to hover long."

She winged closer to the surface of the water. The people aboard the *Hákyrling* were observing our approach, some waving, others working the sails to steady the ship's course through the sea. A skiff had been launched, two sailors rowing it out a short distance from the ship.

Marskal unfurled the rope ladder he'd tied up, letting it dangle as Zynda moved into position over the skiff. Her immense wings billowed as she hovered. Marskal grinned at me. "Want me to go first?"

"I got it," I replied, hooking a boot into the foothold and telling myself I simply climbed down from Violet's back. Ten times over and swinging precariously over the sea. I descended as swiftly as I could, aware of Harlan just above me. Strong hands grabbed me as I reached the skiff, lifting me off the ladder and lowering me into the boat. I turned to thank them, the words dying in my mouth as I faced strange Dasnarian men.

The impulse to flee seized me—immediately followed by the fiercer need to draw my blades and cut them down.

Then Harlan was beside me with a steadying arm. "Sit. It's better for the balance."

I thumped my rear end down, and gave myself a stern talking to. This would be a disaster of a journey if I panicked every time I met a strange Dasnarian man.

Marskal leapt into the skiff and the rope ladder vanished—as did Zynda. I gaped at the empty sky. "Where did she go?"

"She's still there. Just much smaller," Marskal replied with a wink as he sat. A moment later, a jewel bright hummingbird whizzed up and landed on his shoulder. "And here she is. She'll need a moment to rest before she rejoins us in human form."

It was a short row to the *Hákyrling*, and we climbed one more rope ladder up the side of the ship. Harlan went first this time, no doubt to test Kral's temper, and Zynda zipped up to the deck. Enviable, to be able to skip the ladder. My shoulders were feeling the unusual work, and I reminded them that we'd have to climb at least once more.

I took my time, to baby my climbing muscles, to let Harlan say whatever he planned to say, and to absorb the fact that it seemed I recognized the scent of Dasnaria. The *Hákyrling* had been sailing outside of Dasnaria for some time from what they'd told me, so it shouldn't smell like my homeland. And yet... it did. In some gut-penetrating combination of memory and subconscious sensory recognition, the very wood of the side of the ship seemed achingly familiar.

It struck my heart with a thousand emotions at once, none of them I could afford to have. I had a job to do. Later I could wallow in my feelings about it.

I reached the railing and Harlan waited for me, offering a big hand to help me over. Though I didn't need assistance—my shoulder muscles weren't that tired—I grabbed hold and let him pull me up. It felt good, steadying, to have the physical contact with him.

"You're pale," he said quietly. "How are you holding up?"

"Just stop me if I lose my nerve and try to hurl myself overboard," I muttered back.

He chuckled. "You have more courage than a hundred Dasnarian warriors. If it helps, Kral is nervous, too."

I didn't know if that helped, but I forced myself to walk the few steps with Harlan and lift my gaze to Kral's face.

Though I'd known better, I'd had his image in my mind still as the cocky and arrogant seventeen-year-old imperial prince with his eye firmly fixed on the throne of the empire. He still possessed plenty of arrogance—perhaps tempered to confidence—but he'd lost the cockiness. Disappointment had aged him, showing in the frown lines of his forehead. His square jaw looked sharper, especially clenched with tension, and his icy blue eyes that had always held such disdain were muddied with emotion. A dark-skinned woman with the athletic build of a knife-fighter and close-cropped hair hovered protectively beside him. In her large, black eyes and the strong lines of her face, I recognized Kaja. This had to be Jepp.

I didn't know who to greet first—or what to say—but Kral saved me the trouble. He drew his sword, then dropped to his knees so swiftly I didn't have time to flinch or draw my daggers. Jepp had her blades in each hand, reacting with lightning speed, but stayed where she was. Kral held up his broadsword on open palms, bowing his head.

"Jenna, my sister," he said in a carrying voice—and I became aware that all activity had stilled to observe the moment. "I offer the *bjoja at satt*. I owe you a life. For all the wrongs I've done you,

I offer my life to you."

I almost couldn't breathe through the shock. I knew of the *bjoja at satt*, the ritual offering of recompense—mainly from the epic ballads we'd sing in the seraglio—but had never witnessed it. Men only offered this level of reconciliation to another man. According to the tales, if I accepted his offer, I could take his sword and use it to behead him and he wouldn't lift a finger to resist. Never mind that I couldn't swing a sword of that weight with any grace—I could use it well enough to kill him.

Jepp looked alarmed, and justifiably so. Her sharp gaze met mine, and I wondered what she'd do to me if I took Kral's life. Harlan went to her, speaking softly in her ear, and she visibly sagged, resigned grief filling her. She met my gaze again, pressed her lips together, and inclined her head in acceptance.

"It's your right," Harlan said to me, loudly enough for everyone to hear. "Kral has made the *bjoja at satt*, the traditional offer of reparation, and you are within your rights to accept. No one will blame you if you do."

I gazed down at Kral, who hadn't moved, though holding up the weight of that sword at that angle had to be a strain. Vengeful Jenna stirred in me, full of vicious, agonizing hate, ready to seize the blade and exact revenge. So many times I'd imagined a vengeance like this: Kral groveling in apology, at my mercy. So many times I'd awakened from nightmares of blood and Dasnarian soldiers falling to my blade and fury.

Some of the dreams had been real.

I didn't have clear memories of the night I killed my late ex-husband and of his men. Fragments emerges in those bad dreams, however. Some of those images I knew must be brutalized Jenna's fantasies of revenge, as she craved more murder. It sickened me to know I carried that inside me.

It also filled me with anger, though a cleaner kind of rage

this time. Danu's high sun beat down on me. The goddess of the bright blade and unflinching justice had come to me through the woman who was the long-dead mother of another warrior woman, staring at me as I held her husband's life in my hands. There were no shadows to this decision. Danu's clear sight filled me, and I took Kral's offered sword.

It was heavier than I'd imagined, the balance all wrong for me as I wrapped my hands around the thick hilt. But I had the strength now. All the years of training served me well. No longer weak, I lifted the blade. No one moved to stop me, the only sounds the snap of a sail, the creak of the wood, and the calls of the seabirds chasing the ship.

I took a step to position myself, and Jepp tensed, then forced herself still. Summoning all the strength I'd trained into my body, I braced, raised the sword higher—and hurled it over the side and into the sea.

~ 7 ~

"**G**ET UP," I said to Kral, my voice as imperiously icy as Ochieng had ever accused me of being. *No princess,* Kaja's voice echoed, and as I met her daughter's eyes, I remembered how that advice had been to hide me. Now I was done hiding, and sometimes being a princess was necessary.

This would be one of those times.

"Stand and be a man," I said to Kral in Dasnarian, deliberately needling him. He rose to his feet, strong and tall, blue eyes wary. "How dare you," I sneered at him, letting my anger shine. "You want to paint more blood on my hands, hang the responsibility for your death around my neck? Leave me to face your grieving widow? That is no reparation. You're sorry for the part you played in what happened to me? Then live and make things right again."

To my surprise, Jepp nodded. "That is Danu's way," she said, in reasonably good Dasnarian. "Your death serves no one, but a life well lived tips the scales back to justice."

I nodded back. Then she turned and kicked Kral in the shin with a hard-tipped boot. He flinched and scowled at her. "That stung, *hystrix.*"

"I sure hope so," she fired back. "What in Danu's tits were you thinking, springing that shit on me?"

"It's between me and Jenna—and I knew you'd try to talk

me out of it."

"Ivariel," I corrected, lifting my chin when he gave me a puzzled frown. "I left Jenna behind in a waterfront inn in Sjør, along with the diamond ring that had wedded her to a monster. She stayed in that room where she'd been left alone because her captor figured her for too stupid and timid to leave on her own via an open window. But I took her dancer's legs and silent grace to elude you, Kral. Jenna was uneducated, but I have learned, so many things. I am Ivariel."

Kral eyed me with new glimmers of respect. Then he bowed to me, as he would to another man. "I greet you, Ivariel, who I recognize as my full-blood sister. Many years have passed—too many—and no apology is enough for what I did to you, and for what I stood by and allowed our family to do you, but I've forfeited the ambition that drove me. I understand you're looking to put things right again, and I'm at your service."

"We both are," Jepp put in, laying a hand on his arm. "Where Kral goes, I go—and I claim a friendship with your sisters, Inga and Helva, and with other women of the palace. My blades are in your service."

A relief washed through me that I hadn't expected. Nobody expected me to forgive Kral, and that made my path forward much easier. "I accept your help and your blades," I replied formally.

Kral glanced wistfully at the sea. "Except I'm down a blade. Did you really have to throw it overboard? That was a really good sword."

Shockingly, I nearly laughed. By the twitch of Harlan's mouth, he suppressed laughter, too. And I suddenly understood how Harlan had managed to forgive Kral. Our brother truly had changed, finding a new humility, a humor that made him more human. And I remembered, too, that Kral had been molded and warped to fit Hulda's ambitions as surely as I had.

I lifted a shoulder and let it fall. "Better to lose your sword than your head, brother."

Everyone relaxed. Marskal and Zynda edged into the previously tense circle. Zynda looked perfectly lovely and human—as if she'd never been anything else—her long, black hair coiled up and held in place with jeweled pins, her blue silk gown pristine. She glanced up at a whoosh of wings, and Zyr landed on a cleared space of deck, running a few steps to burn off the speed. Once he came to a halt, Karyn dismounted and Zyr became a man, neatly dressed, long hair tied back.

The shapeshifting thing made my head hurt, my mind somehow not quite able to keep up with the shift in reality.

"You get more used to it," Jepp said beside me in Common Tongue. She smiled thinly when I started. I'd have to get used to these silent-footed warrior women, too. "Over time," she clarified, "your brain quits trying to see the change from one thing to the other and you just accept that the hummingbird is now your gorgeous friend." She eyed me, then thrust out a hand. "I'm Jepp."

Since I knew that, I took this for a more formal introduction. "I'm Ivariel."

She nodded thoughtfully, studying me. "I've heard a lot about you—at least, about you as a girl. Kral said you were stunningly beautiful and I thought he exaggerated, but no. You might be the most beautiful woman I've ever laid eyes on."

"Even compared to Queen Amelia?" I asked, amused and more than a little taken aback. The seraglio of the Imperial Palace had concentrated the most beautiful women of the Dasnarian Empire—and I'd never seen anyone as lovely as Amelia.

Jepp dashed her hand to the side. "Eh, that's magic. You get used to that sheen of the goddess around her after a while, too. But you—you're the real thing. That hair of yours, it really *does* look like ivory."

"I'm the product of meticulous breeding," I replied, hearing the bitterness in my own voice. "Like a racehorse or a hunting hound, I was carefully bred over generations to be decorative, and pleasing to the male eye."

"The female eye, too," she replied with a flirtatious smile.

"Jepp, don't hit on my sister," Kral said, sounding both annoyed and amused.

Jepp winked at me saucily. "Your brother has this monogamy thing, and I've promised to go along with it, so I'm really not making an offer." She leaned in to whisper. "But if I *were* free…"

I laughed, and her grin widened. Kral and Harlan, standing together, watched us with cautious smiles, too. Sobering, I said, "I knew your mother. Did they tell you?"

She stilled, cocked her head as if hearing a distant sound. "No. And Andi spoke to me this morning to warn of your arrival. She might have mentioned that."

"I think she knew I wanted to be the one to tell you." I took a breath. "Kaja saved my life."

"Will you tell me about her?" Jepp asked quietly. "I was a girl when she died."

"I know. She was so proud of you, her Jesperanda."

Jepp's mouth twisted even as her eyes shone with unshed tears. "You did know her. She was the only one to call me that."

"Yes, I met her on the ship I took to escape Dasnaria. More to the point, she cornered me. She taught me how to hold a blade, how to adapt my dances for fighting, and simple things like counting and how to stop being so afraid. When we reached the Port of Ehas, she took me to the Temple of Danu and gave me my first sword. Your mother was my first and best friend—

and she saved me in every way possible."

"That sounds like Mom," Jepp replied in a hushed tone. "Thank you for this gift."

"Thank you, for lending me your mother."

She nodded, eyes bright. "Should we hug?" she asked. "I feel like we should hug."

I laughed, feeling watery also, and opened my arms. She seized me in a tight embrace, then kissed the side of my neck, bared by my upswept braids. "Thank you," she said again, then released me.

Stepping back, she surveyed the gathering. "So, if we're done with nobly sacrificing our lives and getting weepy over people long dead, can we get to the business of talking war?"

Oh yes, she was definitely Kaja's daughter.

"YOU CAN'T BE serious about sailing an army of elephants to Dasnaria," Kral declared, scowling at me.

We sat around a table in the captain's dining room, the woodwork inlaid with a master carpenter's hand. Ochieng possessed considerable skill in the art, so I knew enough to recognize a master at work—even though this style was distinctly Dasnarian. Another disconcerting mix of feelings washed over me as those two worlds overlapped, my recent past mingling with the distant past to make for an unsettling present. I'd left Dasnaria knowing so little about my country outside my small cage, and now I returned much wiser and more experienced—and yet most things of the empire were new to me.

I raised a brow at Kral's challenging statement, oddly reassured by his arrogant behavior, so much more familiar than the humble, apologetic Kral. "I am absolutely serious. My husband Ochieng grew up training elephants. When the barrier expanded to include Nyambura, flooding us with magic, his native talent blossomed into a magical ability to care for and sustain the elephants. He can keep them sufficiently warm."

Kral waved that away. "Eh, it's summer in Dasnaria right now, just as it is here. Warmth isn't the concern."

I blinked at that, realigning my assumptions. Until my wedding, I'd lived all my life in the cloistered confines of the seraglio at the Imperial Palace. When I left on my wedding journey, a week after my eighteenth birthday, it had been bitter winter outside. Somehow I'd always thought of Dasnaria as eternally covered in deep snow, bitterly cold, with overcast skies only occasionally parting to reveal a distant sun in pale skies. A flush of shame roiled my stomach at the reminder of pitiful, stupid Jenna, who hadn't had the wit to recognize Dasnaria had seasons, too.

Harlan, across from me, watched me with steady gray eyes, perhaps guessing at my embarrassment. He didn't say anything, but gave me a moment to regain my poise by turning to Kral. "Don't dance around the issue, shark," he said. "Just spit out your concern."

Kral gestured around him with an incredulous expression. "Have you forgotten where you come from, rabbit? We're talking about invading the fucking Dasnarian Empire! The closest port to the Imperial Palace is Jofarrstyr, which is heavily fortified. Then it's a journey of several hours—at a good clip—to reach the Imperial Palace, which is impregnable."

"It is," Jepp put in, looking around the table. "Of all of us, only Kral, Harlan, Ivariel and I have been there and—"

"I don't count," I interrupted.

She closed her open mouth, giving me a fierce glare. "Don't

ever say you don't count. You absolutely matter, to everyone in this room, and more."

"I mean," I said gently, "that my experience with the Imperial Palace is quite limited. I only left the seraglio for my wedding and a few associated events. When I departed on my wedding journey, I was secluded in an enclosed carriage. The entourage paused for me to have one look at the Imperial Palace—the famous view, from the end of the lake," I added for Karyn's benefit, and she smiled nostalgically. "That's the one time I've seen the palace from the outside. That is why it's not useful to count me as someone who knows the place," I said to Jepp, giving her a wry look. "Ironically enough, *you* know the place of my birth better than I do."

Unabashed, she gazed back thoughtfully. "Just as you knew my mother better than I did, at least as adult to adult."

That hadn't occurred to me, and I nodded solemnly. How oddly like mirrors we were, Jepp and I, connected by so many threads. Time enough to muse over that later. "Kral makes an excellent point," I said, making myself look at him—and savoring the surprise in his glacier blue eyes. "Even with the elephants, our warriors, and those troops Her Majesty the High Queen might agree to lend, we don't have enough might to take Jofarrstyr, much less the forces I assume would be positioned against us on the road to the Imperial Palace. Also, most of those people are innocent of wrongdoing. It's Hestar and Hulda we want." Even Kral acknowledged the truth of that. "I also understand that you and our allies don't have the might to defeat the navy currently mustered and circling us in this storm?" I asked Kral.

He jerked his chin in annoyed confirmation. "I understand Nakoa is letting the storm disperse even now, which will leave the *Hákyrling* and the few other ships with us surrounded, just a few morsels of juicy bait for those circling ships."

"Diverting weather takes tremendous magical effort," Zynda said to Kral. "Nakoa has sustained your impasse as long as he could." She appeared to be languidly relaxed in her chair, but I caught the terse edge to her voice. As did Kral.

"*Your* impasse, too, shapeshifter," Kral growled. "I seem to recall that we have been out here buying time for you, so your precious Annfwn wouldn't be overwhelmed by two enemies at once."

"Don't pretend you did it for us, beetle man," Zyr sneered, tipping his chair back onto two legs and balancing precariously. "We know your motivations."

"Beetle man?" I asked, partly because I really wanted to know, but also to diffuse the building argument.

Zyr glanced at me, sharp humor in his deep blue eyes. "In their armor, they look like giant beetles, don't you think?"

I passed a hand over my mouth to cover the snicker— because he was absolutely right about Dasnarian armor—and Karyn poked Zyr in the ribs. "Behave," she hissed.

He snuck a kiss, moving fast enough that I almost thought he'd shapeshifted, and grinned at her scowl. "You know you love it when I'm *irreverent*."

I thought I had the meaning of the word—as they were using Common Tongue along with the rest of us for this discussion—but Karyn blushed so deeply that I wondered.

"Kral is our ally as much as anyone," Jepp put in crisply, casting a quelling glare liberally around the table. "And Her Majesty appointed Kral general of her forces, so unless someone wants to cross blades with Ursula, I suggest we dispense with this bickering. What do you propose, Ivariel?"

"So," I said, taking the cue, "the storm will disperse in an-other couple of days. Our ships cannot stay here for long. We cannot defeat either the Dasnarian Navy currently fielded against us or the empire itself by force. That leaves us guile, cunning, and stealth."

Kral eyed me. "The objective?"

"Liberate our sisters, remove Hestar from the throne, and kill Hulda."

~ 8 ~

"OH, IS THAT all." Kral threw up a hand in a dramatic gesture. "What are we waiting for then? Let's just skip off, do that, and be back in time for supper."

"You asked for an objective," I pointed out sweetly, "not the strategy."

"I asked for a rational plan," he shot back, "not a fantasy of vengeance."

"Be careful, shark," I warned in Dasnarian. "I may have declined your sacrifice, but I reserve the right to exact any vengeance that occurs to me."

Harlan looked between us, quietly measuring. "I'd never realized how alike you two are," he commented, also in Dasnarian, smiling broadly when we both turned icy glares on him. He held up his hands in peace. "Don't gut the messenger."

Kral and I exchanged assessing looks. We hadn't been close as children. As full brother and sister born only a year apart, we'd been naturally competitive. Something, I realized, Hulda had encouraged. Hestar, born two weeks after I was, to our father's second wife, had been my closest playmate. We'd looked so alike that the ladies of the seraglio had called us twins. Until we'd been forcibly divided, molded into our separate and disparate gender roles, we'd been great companions, very alike in our imagined games. There had been a time I thought we'd have that forever.

Then he was groomed to be emperor and I was sold off to be chewed up and discarded.

But Kral and I... we'd ended up on similar paths. Both of us exiles and rebels. In his face, I saw my own. The same hardness, the same yearning for more.

"I say we concoct a strategy to infiltrate the Imperial Palace and execute a coup from within," I offered, switching back to Common Tongue. "I bet you know the defenses of the place like the back of your hand, Brother."

"I did before," he admitted. "They might have changed."

I shook my head. "Dasnaria is not a place of rapid change."

"And Hestar is not a man to change things," Harlan put in. "He worshipped our loathsome father and emulates him in all ways."

"Besides, why change what has worked for hundreds of years?" Kral said in wry agreement. "All right then, yes I know the defenses."

"I memorized quite a bit of the layout in my time there," Jepp added.

"The knowledge won't help us much as there's only one way in and out of the Imperial Palace," Kral mused, then glanced at me. "You'll recall going through all the stages and checkpoints along the long drawbridge."

I nodded, not saying I didn't remember anything much except pain and the haze of the dulling opos smoke.

"Then there's the Imperial Palace guard," Kral continued. "A small army right there."

"I have another, secret army inside," I said, and Kral frowned, perplexed. "The women of the seraglio can help us," I clarified.

A thick silence fell, and it was Karyn who broke it. "But will they?" she asked.

"They certainly have good reason to," Zyr burst out, slamming his chair down onto all four legs and glaring at her.

"Reason isn't enough," she replied calmly, then looked at me. "Remember what that was like, the feeling of terrible danger and the prospect of lifelong isolation for the least step out of line. The women of the seraglio have not lived their lives with even a thought of leaving the Imperial Palace. Most wouldn't dream of contradicting a man, much less rebelling against them."

"Inga and Helva would," Jepp put in with confidence.

I considered Jepp and Karyn's points while Zyr muttered to himself and Zynda listened with interest. Marskal hadn't said anything, but the thoughts moved behind his quiet brown eyes. Deep waters there. "I haven't seen or talked to my sisters in all these years, so I'll accept your word there, Jepp. I'm not surprised to hear they have spine. And you make a good argument, Karyn, but I have to point out that *you* rebelled, and you left Dasnaria."

She flicked a glance at Kral. "I didn't leave so much as was pushed out of the nest. I have never been one with spine."

"That's absurd," Zyr spat, rounding on her. "You have more spine, more sheer courage than anyone else I know. Maybe you needed the spark that Jepp lit, but you fed it fuel and fanned the flames."

She smiled at him, looking misty, then turned back to me. "A spark, yes. Maybe with the right tinder we can fuel the flames of rebellion buried in their hearts. We know they're not truly happy, and so many of those women nurse black rage deep inside."

That came a bit too close to pitiful Jenna, but I let that slide off. "I've been thinking about what you said, that my story has been an inspiration. If I can sneak into the seraglio, I'll light that fire. I just need to get into the palace."

"We've been discussing how that's the difficult part," Kral said, flinging up a hand in exasperation.

"I know how to get us in," Jepp volunteered, grinning at Kral, then at the twin shapeshifters. "We fly."

"Fly?" Kral echoed, while Harlan tipped his head to gaze at the ceiling, running some sort of scenario in his head.

"I noticed it when I was in my special prison cum guest room at the palace," she replied. "Behind some of the locked doors that protect the seraglio, but not *in* the seraglio itself," she clarified for the group. "Because they were pretty sure I was female, but found me just manly enough that they didn't want to risk me in there full time," she added for me.

I could just imagine what my people had made of the brash, quick-bladed warrior woman. Come to that, I wondered what they'd make of me. I'd been so long in the world, living a life of freedom and fighting my own battles that they'd no doubt find me less than feminine anymore. The thought was heartening.

"The tower rooms have windows," Jepp was saying. "Narrow ones, and glazed, but big enough to let a person through and they don't even have bars or grates on them, because apparently the lunkheaded Dasnarians can't imagine an aerial attack. We don't have to fuck around with swimming that dismal lake or trying to navigate the multiple segments and guard stations on the drawbridge of doom—or all those archers on the cleared areas around the lake. Zynda and Zyr fly us in, drop us off on a tower, we scamper down to the seraglio." She dusted her hands together. "Boom! Done."

Marskal cleared his throat. "I hate to immediately shoot down a proposed plan, but I feel I have to note that Zynda in dragon form is rather… noticeable."

"And there are plenty of archers on the towers and parapets ready to literally shoot anyone down. Or any*thing*," Kral put in, giving Jepp an arrogant smile. "That's why no one worries about an aerial attack."

"I have excellent vision," she retorted. "I counted your archers and manifold guard on the towers and parapets—and I also noticed they were all looking down, not up."

"When a big scary dragon flies in overhead, you can be sure they'll be looking up," he shot back.

"Mere arrows cannot penetrate my scales," Zynda declared loftily.

"Yes, but they penetrate my soft hide just fine," I retorted. "It would be better not to sound an alarm, so we need the guards to be looking down." Harlan leveled his gaze on me, nodding, as if he'd come to the same conclusion.

"A distraction." Zyr uncoiled his long body in a shiver of relish. "I do love me a big distraction."

Kral threw up his hands. "It's going to have to be a spectacular distraction to pull all the guards off the walls and make it so no one happens to notice a dragon three times the size of this ship dropping people off on a tower of the Imperial Palace."

"I am a very deep blue, nearly black at night," Zynda said, "and I can glide in silently. Tonight is the new moon, so it will be as dark as it gets. It wouldn't take long to drop off Ivariel."

"And me," Jepp put in firmly, giving me a fierce look. "I can be your guide and back up."

"And me," Karyn echoed. "I can help talk to the women of the seraglio. This is something I need to do," she said to Zyr when he opened his mouth to protest. He closed his mouth with a rueful snap, then took her hand and kissed it.

"Wait," I said, holding up a hand in a gesture I'd use to stop a charging elephant. "You all are talking about going *tonight?*"

"Today, really," Kral replied as if it were a reasonable answer, "as it will take us some time to get there. Element of surprise works for us, as Hestar and our revered brothers will think we're still pinned down by their navy."

"And deposing the leaders will hopefully nullify the navy's orders by the time the storm clears," Jepp added. "Has to be tonight."

Ochieng believed I'd be back in a few hours—and Ursula!—she would *not* be pleased at this change of plans. She'd wanted me to take Harlan with me, but not like this, I was certain. Harlan caught my eye and grimaced ruefully.

"If we're deposing Hestar, we have to put someone in his place," Kral said thoughtfully.

"Do we?" Jepp shot back.

"A vacuum will only suck someone else into the role," he pointed out. "It would be irresponsible of us to leave it to whichever dog fights hardest for the bone."

"Oh, well, we wouldn't want to be irresponsible," she replied, oozing sarcasm, and I sensed her worry beneath it.

Kral looked between me and Harlan. "It would be best to choose our replacement, someone amenable to being allies with the Thirteen Kingdoms and our other friends."

"You always wanted it," Harlan said blandly.

Kral still didn't look at the visibly seething Jepp. "Yes. Yes, I did. I waited many years for an opportunity like this."

"Ivariel is firstborn, however," Harlan commented. Jepp straightened, a funny look on her face, and she stared at me as if suddenly remembering something.

Kral eyed me. "Empress of Dasnaria—why not? Hulda would be so proud to see her prized progeny poised to take the throne after all."

"Except she'll be dead," I replied. "How about we see to that and deposing Hestar before we reorganize the government of the empire?"

"Agreed," Kral said. "All right, so the ladies get dropped off by Zynda, infiltrate the seraglio, while the rest of us create a distraction. That doesn't get the rest of us into the palace, however."

"And we might need help getting out of the seraglio again," I said. "It's set up to allow the women out only accompanied by guard, and I doubt that's changed."

"It hasn't," Jepp and Karyn said at once, grinning at each other for the chorus.

"I can drop the *seraglio team* off," Zynda said, casting a pointed frown at Kral, "then come get all of you and drop you inside the walls."

"Me, Kral, and Harlan at once is more weight than you've carried before," Marskal said, giving her a concerned frown.

"You're skinny," Zyr noted, looking Marskal over. "I'll carry you and Zynda can take the overmuscled Dasnarians."

Kral considered. "It could work. We need to flesh out the details, of course, but sunset is about five hours later there, which gives us some wiggle room. How long to fly us there?"

"I don't know," Zynda replied blandly, "as I've never been to the Imperial Palace."

Jepp chewed on her lip. "Knowing how long it took you to fly here from Annfwn, I'm going to guess a six-hour flight." She glanced at Kral. "Sunrise comes early still this time of year. I say we go for the small hours between midnight and dawn, when the guard will be sleepy and complacent—and everyone else hopefully asleep."

Kral nodded, calculating. "We need to leave in about four hours then. That gives us time to thrash out the plan."

"Make that three hours," Karyn said. "Zyr can't fly as fast as Zynda can."

Zyr scowled and stuck out his tongue at Zynda. "At least I'm not a gruntling."

"Jealous," Zynda replied with breezy venom.

"Neither of you should be taking on a long flight on top of the effort to get us here," Marskal pointed out.

Zynda and Zyr exchanged saucy smiles, temporarily united. "I can do it," Zynda said.

"No problem," Zyr chimed in.

Marskal and Karyn wore identical expressions of resigned exasperation.

"If I may point out a flaw in this plan," I inserted, and they all frowned at me, "you've effectively planned for how Zynda and Zyr will carry us into the Imperial Palace, but how do you plan to get all five humans on the backs of two shapeshifters on the long flight to Dasnaria?"

~ *9* ~

I MIGHT'VE LAUGHED at the appalled looks on their faces, except that Kral shocked me by tossing a salute in my direction, respect in his face. "I am chagrined to find your planning ability outstrips mine, my canny sister."

"I'm accustomed to planning campaigns where distributing people and supplies on animals is a key consideration," I explained, feeling unduly flustered by the compliment. Then I realized my gaffe. "Not that you are animals," I hastily reassured Zyr and Zynda, then winced, because that didn't sound any better.

"Zyr is," Karyn volunteered, squeaking as he pinched her under the table.

Zynda rolled her eyes. "No offense taken. And you're right. I don't think I could carry four of you that far. I do, however, have an idea." She turned a charming smile on Marskal. "We could ask Kiraka to help."

He groaned, rubbing a hand over the back of his neck. "The last thing I want to do is ask that old bitch of a dragon for a favor. Her favors don't come cheap."

"She wants retribution for Hulda's role in unleashing the High Priestess on the people of n'Andana," Zynda argued. "I think she'll do it for free. We can ask Andi to talk her into it. It would be helpful to have Andi ready to magically assist, too, just in case."

"You know what's odd?" Jepp said conversationally. "When I was a prisoner in the Imperial Palace and facing that travesty of a 'trial' before Hestar and the Domstyrr, I kind of lost my temper, and—"

"That sounds like every day to me," Kral inserted, "not remotely odd."

She rolled her eyes. "*Anyway*, Hestar was taunting me about rape and cutting off my pink bits, blah, blah, blah, and—"

"Wait." Kral growled the word, gone from teasing to furious in a heartbeat. "You never told me that part."

"Well, no, because I—silly me—thought you might lose your shit and go storming off and get yourself killed trying to punish him. It didn't happen. See? I'm fine."

She held his gaze, stroking his arm, and I observed her technique with visceral recognition. Talking Kral down, exactly as Ochieng did with me. My brother and I, perhaps much too much alike.

"I wanted to scare Hestar, unsettle him, so I told him that Harlan had given me a message—about Jenna."

Harlan startle in his chair. "I never spoke to you of her."

"I know, I know, but Inga and Helva did. I was lying my ass off, stalling. But I told Hestar that you'd set Jenna up as a queen in a foreign land, where she commanded armies of shape-shifters. I don't know what all I said, but I do recall mentioning that dragons flew at her bidding and sorcerers worked powerful magics for her. And that she was coming for Hestar, to kill him and all of his children, then would take her rightful place as Empress."

A fraught silence fell, and Jepp grinned triumphantly. "Am I psychic or what?" She gestured to me. "Here is Jenna, Queen Ivariel of Nyambura."

"If you'd seen Nyambura, you'd know that isn't saying much," I replied, still struggling with the shock of Jepp's words.

"Details. You *are* commanding dragons, shapeshifters, and sorcerers, and coming to kill Hestar and take his throne."

Definitely a stretch. "I would never kill his children."

"Will you put Hestar's heir on the throne?" Kral asked. "I can tell you that Hestar has been molding the boy in his own image."

I rubbed my forehead. "I don't know. And I refuse to decide anything right now. Let's focus on the immediate task."

"I guess that means it's time to play messenger pigeon," Jepp said grimly. She caught my concerned look and shook it off. "Don't mind me. It's really not that bad, it's just creepy having her in my head. Like an itch I can't scratch."

Kral ran a finger down the bare skin of her arm, giving her such a warm, sympathetic smile that I wondered if someone hadn't simply killed off my seventeen-year-old brother and replaced him with someone else. It happened all the time in tragic Dasnarian legends, so why not? It seemed like a much more rational explanation.

"You don't have to," he told her softly. "We can send a bird."

"Nah. I can do it. Not like I'm going into battle bare-assed or something. Besides, she's been popping in periodically to check on you all, because Ursula is a mother hen." She pointed at me. "And if you tell Her Majesty I said that, I'll cut off your pretty braids."

"Noted," I replied. "Would you pass along a message Ochieng? And I'll need to explain to Ayela and the children. I can write it out."

"You can?" Kral asked, surprised.

"I haven't been sitting on my hands the last two decades,

shark," I answered him. "I've learned to read and write in a couple of languages, and it turns out I'm quite good at math."

Jepp had raised her brows, giving him an "I told you so" look, so he held up his palms to ward us off. "No need to fling eye-daggers at me," he laughed. "I'll need to fill Her Majesty in on the logistics, too."

"And I," Harlan said, rubbing a hand over his forehead. "I'll need to try to explain that—"

"All right, folks," Jepp cut him off, "this is getting to be a lot of messages, so this is what we're going to do. Next time Andi pops in, I'm going to get the request for Kiraka underway, since she'll need to fly here. Then I'll tell her to fetch Ursula, then Ivariel's family. Instead of you all giving me messages, I'll let Andi talk through me. You'll still be passing through her, but that cuts out at least one translator."

"She can do that?" I asked. "That does sound creepy."

"Right?" Jepp shook her head. "Anyone else who wants to pass messages back, put in your requests now."

WHILE I WAITED for my turn to "talk" to Ochieng and the kids, I found a quiet spot on the deck and began running some knife forms. The physical ritual of the exercises soothed my agitated mind, and helped to bleed off some of the emotions crowding my heart. I only hoped Ochieng would understand that I hadn't planned to sneak off to do this on my own.

I finished with Danu's salute—not perfectly executed, as the sun had lowered to mid-afternoon and the surrounding storm made the waters choppy enough to challenge my balance on the pitching deck—and lowered my blades to find Harlan quietly watching nearby. He offered me a towel to dry the sweat from my face. That was my baby brother: still taking care of me.

"Essla does that form," he commented. "Or one like it."

"I've bastardized it over the years," I admitted. "It's got a lot more of the ducerse in it than a true follower of Danu would use."

"Depends on what you think makes someone a true follower," he countered. "I'd argue that it's far more important to cleave to the principles the goddess embodies than stick to the appearance of practice. In fact, it's when people start performing their worship for others, doing it for show and abandoning the values of the religion or philosophy, that corruption occurs."

"I think you're right, but I had no idea you'd become such a deep thinker."

He smiled without humor. "You're not the only one who spent the last couple of decades educating yourself. After you... left, and then after I was exiled myself, I spent a lot of time trying to understand how our family and country could have become so twisted."

I rubbed the towel over the back of my neck and leaned on the rail, looking over the water. The magic made for a strange sight, the storm a churning wall in all directions, while we and a few other ships sailed under clear skies.

"I think it's power," I told him, as he leaned his forearms on the rail, too. "Maybe people aren't meant to have so much power. It's like an infection that slowly spreads through their minds and makes them unable to think rationally anymore."

He nodded thoughtfully. "I've certainly witnessed many instances of power corrupting rulers."

"Your Ursula seems to have escaped the insidious creep of it." At least, so far.

"'So far,'" he added my unspoken words for me. "And yes,

we're both aware of that danger. Essla maybe more than anyone, as she fears becoming her father."

I could understand that. "I am far more like my mother than I want to be."

"You're nothing like Hulda," he said with grim certainty. "Never think it."

"You don't know," I replied, fixing my eyes on the water. "I have terrible things in me, Harlan. I killed Rodolf."

He jerked, swinging his head to me. "He found you?" Harlan sounded so horrified, so aghast on my behalf that I felt like I should comfort him, but I didn't know how. Or if I even could.

"Yes. He tracked me almost to Nyambura. He even brought the Arynherk diamond I left at the inn in Sjør."

Harlan was gripping the rail, knuckles white. "Kral gave it to Hestar, but when Rodolf disappeared..." He blew out a long breath. "I looked for you. I never stopped looking."

"I know you did." I had known, in my bones, that Harlan would search for me. For so many years, when the trade caravans resumed after the rainy season, part of me half-expected Harlan to turn up. But he never had, and after a while, I stopped thinking that he might.

"No, I mean, I *looked*," he ground out, anguish in his voice. He laughed humorlessly. "I thought I looked in every place that had elephants because I knew you'd find them. By the time I met Essla... I don't want you to think I pledged the *Elskathorrl* to her lightly. I knew it meant I'd..."

"Given up on finding me," I finished for him. I turned to look at him, set a hand on his shoulder. "Harlan it had been so long. Of course you had to put an end to it."

"Did I?" He shook his head, disgust on his face. "*He* found you, which meant I could have, if only I'd tried harder."

"Rodolf found me after a few months, because he had a

fresh trail," I told him. "When he tracked me, you were probably still a virtual prisoner at the Imperial Palace."

He jerked his head in a nod. "For the better part of a year."

"Rodolf arrived just before the rains did. After I killed him, we made sure the rains washed away all trace of him and his men. Their bones lie deep beneath the hard-packed earth, unmarked and unmourned."

"Good." Harlan still wasn't looking at me, but neither did he shake off my hand, so I edged closer and stroked his back, somewhat amused to find myself soothing him over this after all.

"How did you kill him?" he asked.

I hesitated, not really wanting to expose the monster inside myself. Harlan turned his head to look at me finally, his gray eyes assessing. "If it's too painful to speak of, you don't have to tell me, but if you can—I'd really like to know."

"You might be sorry you asked," I said, trying to be teasing and failing utterly as my voice creaked.

He put his hand over mine on the rail, covering and enfolding it as he looked steadily into my eyes. "Never. You can tell me anything."

"You've grown into such a fine man," I marveled. "You were a good-hearted boy, but you're even better now. I'm amazed that you could, coming from what we did."

"You did, too," he replied. "You have found your place as an embodiment of Danu's ideals. You are clear-eyed and act in the name of justice, protecting the weak and defending those who can't defend themselves."

"You can't know that."

"I can," he replied solemnly.

"I'm not always that. Killing Rodolf—there was nothing clear-minded or just about that."

"Tell me."

~ 10 ~

I TOOK A breath, steadying myself to find the words to speak of something I hadn't in so long. "When Kaja found me, I was so broken. I knew nothing about the outside world—not even stupid little things like that I could open the portholes in my cabin or light the lantern, so I sat in the dark."

"How could you know?" he asked.

"I know I couldn't have, but I was so helpless, on top of being injured. Kaja taught me how to defend myself. Remember that little dagger you gave me?"

"An eating knife," he agreed. "So many times over the years I wished I'd thought to give you more weapons, spent more time teaching you to use them."

"I wasn't ready. Remember that I slept most of the time, with all the blood loss, and other damage. And we never imagined I'd be going alone."

"No. You shouldn't have had to." He looked over the sea and I knew he'd never forgive himself that Kral found us.

"None of us can change the past," I said softly, giving his back one last pat and turning to look out to sea beside him, adding my hand to the stack over his.

"True words," he agreed. "So, Kaja taught you what I didn't."

"Yes. And she helped me create... a veneer, I guess. I layered Priestess Ivariel over broken Jenna, sealing up all those cracks. I colored my hair, darkened my skin, took vows of silence and celibacy, so no one would hear my accent or trip over how very messed up I was sexually."

He made a snorting sound, but didn't comment.

"And it mostly worked. But when Ivariel learned to wield a sword and blades, so did Jenna, and she... Jenna is not rational." I paused, but he didn't argue with me that we were the same person, as many people might attempt to do. "On the caravan road, a man tried to rob me. I don't remember it, but I came back to myself with him in ribbons."

"He deserved it."

"Did he? I meted out vengeance, not justice."

"Sometimes they're the same."

"Sometimes they aren't. With Rodolf... I don't remember much of that night either. I went to him, to keep him away from Ochieng and the D'tiembos."

"He let you go alone?"

"I snuck out without telling him," I confessed, "because he wouldn't have sanctioned it. But I couldn't bear to see them hurt. They would have defended me, those kind people who'd opened their home to me. They didn't deserve being attacked by the beetle men."

Harlan breathed a laugh at that, which gave me the heart to go on. "Rodolf, he attempted to assert his marital rights, and Jenna... Well, she awakened and she took him apart. Many of his men, too. I don't know how many men I killed that night."

"All of them, apparently," Harlan noted, no reproach in his voice.

"No, because Ochieng and the D'tiembos brought the elephants. They were the ones to finish what crazed Jenna started. They cleaned up the mess. I woke up much later—I nearly died of my wounds—and so I mostly know the story from what Ochieng has told me."

Harlan made a thoughtful sound, glanced at me as he squeezed my hand. "Thank you for telling me. I'm not sorry you killed him."

"I'm not either, but..." I wrestled with how much to tell him.

"But you're afraid it will happen again, when we reach Dasnaria."

I blew out a long, cleansing breath, beyond grateful that he'd said it. "Exactly."

"The red rage is a part of the Konyngrr family tradition," he said, surprising me. "Did you know that?"

"No! I mean, it has a name?"

"It does. The battle fury that consumes a warrior, makes them nearly unstoppable. They don't feel wounds, often don't remember what occurs. It makes sense that you wouldn't have heard the stories, as I doubt the women would've retold them, if they even knew. But when I began training, they warned me about the red rage. More, they encouraged us to use it. It's said that our ancestor took the throne of Dasnaria largely because he was so fearsome in battle."

I assimilated that with the sense of the world shifting beneath my feet—more than the unsteady sea caused. "I always assumed that insane rage came from what had happened to me."

He lifted a shoulder and let it fall. "That might've helped to trigger it, but it makes sense to me that the Konyngrr women would inherit the trait as easily as the men. The women just had less opportunity to express it."

Or we'd always vented our aggression through cold calculation. Cruelty, manipulation, and poison had been the weapons of the Konyngrr women. And my mother had been the best at all of those twisted skills. "Has the red rage happened to you?"

"A time or two. It can be useful, if you're pointed at the right thing." He canted his head at me. "It allows you to advance without fear."

"Thank you. That is helpful to know."

He smiled at me, a little wistful. "A small thing, but at least something I can give you, after all this time."

"Harlan, you gave me *everything*. You are the reason I had the time, that I had a life at all."

He let go of out handclasp and put an arm around me, pulling me into a one-shouldered embrace. "I'm glad you found Ochieng," he said gruffly. "I worried that, if you lived, that you wouldn't find a way to be… I don't want to say normal, but—"

I interrupted him with a laugh. "I won't ever be normal, but yes—Ochieng gave me the time and space to heal, and he offered me love when I needed it, without expecting anything from me in return. Where you set me free, Ochieng gave me grounding to find myself again."

"Now I understand why you're concerned about explaining to him that you didn't mean to sneak off on your own again."

My heart squeezed. "Yes. I promised I'd never do that to him again. Hopefully he'll understand."

"He seems like the understanding type. My Essla, however…" He blew out a breath. "She may not be so forgiving."

I briefly wrestled with what to say. "You should know—and I'm breaking a confidence here—but she talked to me about that. She suggested that I ask you to go with me to Dasnaria."

He straightened, turning and searching my face. "Come again?"

"I know, it shocked me, too. But that's why she came to find me this morning. She suspected this mission would be difficult for me, that I'd need your support and help, and also that you needed to go back, to tie up your own loose ends."

"She never ceases to amaze me," he said reflectively. "That may be another answer to the conundrum of power. For all of her brusque and decisive ways, Essla is truly selfless. If anything, she forgets to want enough for herself, she's always so intent on protecting everyone else."

"Sound like someone else I know," I said with a smile.

"Yes." He grinned wryly. "She says the same thing."

"So, the question is, once we depose Hestar, who *do* we put on the throne of the Dasnarian Empire?"

He sobered. "Do you want it?"

"I..." I hesitated. "Do you think Jepp has foresight?"

With a deep belly laugh, he shook his head. "No. She is simply a very good bullshitter."

I wondered. "I just haven't thought about it," I said, knowing it wasn't true as I said it.

"You thought about it some." He gave me a keen look. "I saw it in you."

"I am my mother's daughter," I retorted. "Enough that, yes, all right, I thought about it—even wanted it for a few minutes—but I don't know if I want to discover how power might corrupt me."

"Maybe you'd be the right person to wield it. You know what it's like to be powerless."

"True." I turned it over in my mind, but the decision felt too huge. "Kral is the logical choice."

"He won't take it."

I raised a dubious brow and Harlan wagged a finger at me.

"You don't fool me. By the way, I knew you wouldn't kill him."

"I thought I might."

"No you didn't." He grinned at my scowl. "Regardless, Kral

loves Jepp—she saved him from being a monster, and she would be miserable as empress. When he gave it up, he gave it up forever."

"We'll see." Personally, I thought Kral was like me. Hulda had fed us ambition from the cradle on. I doubted Kral would be able to turn it down. "I suppose we can see how Leo, Loke and Mykal turned out," I mused.

"I don't hold out high hopes."

"No." I didn't either. "If we put a child on the throne, that leaves them open to manipulation by the worst elements. We can't do that—not to the kid or the empire."

"We could burn it all down," Harlan suggested, blandly enough that I wasn't sure if he was joking or serious. "Depose Hestar, scatter the Domstyrr, return the empire's holdings to its composite kingdoms and protectorates."

"End the Dasnarian Empire entirely," I breathed, dazzled by the possibilities. What a vengeance that would be. The lost princess returns to the empire that nearly destroyed her and destroys it instead.

"It would be a glorious ending to the tale," he said, still watching me.

"Or a tragic ending."

"Glory or tragedy—both in the eye of the beholder."

"I suppose that's true. I—"

"Come on you two," Kral called from the door to the dining cabin. "Jepp is ready to broker your marital apologies."

"I suppose you'd know all about that," I said, heading that way.

He grimaced ruefully. "You have no idea."

I paused, studying him, beginning to truly see him as is, not as he was. "I like Jepp," I told him, and it felt like a kind of peace offering. "Her mother was one of the best people I've ever known. If Jepp is anything like Kaja…"

"Honest to a fault, afraid of nothing, everything she thinks comes out of her mouth?" Kral asked with a half smile.

"Sounds right." I started to move, then paused again. "I'm glad she saved you."

"Me too, sister of mine. Me too."

Maybe Harlan was right, and Kral wouldn't jump at the chance to be emperor. We would see.

～ 11 ～

KIRAKA ARRIVED LIKE a second sun, blazing gold in the sky. Zynda could hear Kiraka's thoughts and warned us of the dragon's imminent arrival, so we were on deck and ready to go. The guys were rigging another rope ladder for Kiraka to slip over her shoulders, so they could climb up, along with a pulley system to load supplies. Zyr and Karyn had already left, getting a head start to make up for the gríobhth's slower speed. Zynda had sweetly offered for Karyn to ride her or Kiraka, so Zyr wouldn't get too tired, which Zyr had *not* appreciated.

"His gríobhth form is particularly possessive, even territorial," Zynda explained to me. "He can't stand the thought of Karyn riding someone else—he goes a little crazy with it."

"Then why did you poke at him about it?" I wondered.

She widened her big blue eyes in false innocence. "That's my responsibility as a big sister. Don't you torment your little brothers—or rather, didn't you, before?"

"No." I must've been giving her an odd look because a line formed between her winged brows. "I mean, when we were little, maybe, but the boys leave the seraglio around age seven to be raised as men. I didn't see any of them again until I turned eighteen and went out long enough for my wedding festivities. And that was for, like, three events."

She stared at me in consternation, a hint of panic in her face.

"The women don't leave the seraglio *ever*? At *all*?"

"Some do. The wives go out to attend their husbands' beds, same with the concubines and rekjabrel. And the empress goes out to attend court."

"So do Inga and Helva," Jepp chimed in, "and there were some family breakfasts with the wives and kids outside the seraglio when I was there—gender divided, though. And the women could observe court entertainments from behind a screened alcove." She made a face.

"Things *have* opened up considerably," I observed with interest. Inga and Helva's influence, no doubt.

"Are you kidding?" Zynda burst out, expression a little wild. "It sounds like a cage!"

Marskal glanced over, his hands full of rope, looking concerned, but I waved him away. Zynda was only upset on my behalf, I figured. "It *is* a cage," I replied very seriously. "A plush and luxurious one, but a cage nevertheless. That's why I'm going back to break it open."

"I've changed my mind," she bit out, a hint of dragon fire in her voice. "I'm not just dropping you off. I'm going with you."

"Don't fuck up the plan now, shapeshifter." Jepp assessed her friend with a keen eye. "We all know you make a terrible soldier, but if you can't follow the plan, tell us now."

Zynda sulked, there was no other word for it. "Fine," she said. "But if anything goes wrong, I'm burning it all down with dragon fire."

"Innocent people," I reminded her. "There's a reason this is a targeted strike."

"Jepp," Kral shouted, "let's go!"

"See you girls in Dasnaria," Jepp said with a saucy grin, giving us each a kiss on the cheek before she jogged off to leap onto the rope ladder dangling from Kiraka, climbing as agilely as a spider monkey.

"That's my cue," Zynda said. And she was a hummingbird hovering before my eyes. She zipped around my head, then zoomed to the other side of the ship, exploding in midair into the sapphire blue dragon. Kral was climbing up to Kiraka after Jepp, Marskal and Harlan headed my way.

"Ready?" Marskal asked gravely, and I nodded. I was beginning to learn that Ursula's lieutenant was as habitually somber as Ochieng was sunny. He provided a counterbalance to Zynda's wildness in a way that I supposed Ochieng must balance my more dour nature. We hadn't been apart like this in many years, not since I'd gone to Chimto to stop a war. Not that we hadn't been apart for long days of work and sometimes overnight, but not divided by such distance—and I felt more unmoored than I'd expected.

When we "spoke," he'd been understanding, of course, and agreed that the strategy and timing made sense. Oddly, I could hear the cadence of his voice, even relayed by Andi speaking through Jepp. It had been more disconcerting than reassuring, however, the dissonance of not being able to touch him, or feel the subtle shifts of emotion that spoke more clearly than words.

My shoulders groaned at the climb up the rope ladder, and I ruefully reflected that there would be several more in my future. When I touched ground again, it would be in Dasnaria. Again sandwiched between Marskal and Harlan, I braced as Zynda plunged us into the churning storm.

DASNARIA IN LATE summer turned out to be surprisingly lush and beautiful. Though we flew as high up as the dragons could, the features of the land below laid out under us like a colorful map. Harlan shouted in my ear, pointing out the cities and mountains, names I'd memorized along with which family held how much power, but had never laid eyes on.

We'd decided to land at Robsyn, a minor kingdom on the main continent and a calculated risk, but one I'd argued for. Princessa Adaladja of Robsyn had attended my misbegotten wedding celebrations—and had offered me help to escape the marriage to Rodolf. I'd been too obedient, too certain of my doom and the immovability of the bars of the cage that held me, to even contemplate her words. Now I'd redeem that offer, if it was still good. Even Kral had agreed that if anyone would be bold enough to aid us in this treachery toward the empire, it would be Prince Fredrick Robsyn and his unconventional wife.

Fortuitously, though Ada had described their kingdom as distant from the Imperial Palace, it did lie in our flight path. As the dragon flew, it wasn't that far at all, not considering the distance we'd already covered. Besides, we had to land somewhere to reshuffle our passengers, and both Harlan and Kral had seemed certain there weren't any open spaces where the dragons could land unobserved. It seemed odd to me, after the vast plains of Chiyajua, occupied only by grass and wildlife, but Dasnaria was densely populated. It made me even more keenly aware of how lucky Harlan and I had been to make our way through the mountains unseen.

That, and Harlan's cleverness, even as a boy.

Robsyn Castle turned out to be set in a lush and lovely river valley. It had high walls, of course, but they were studded with glowing fires that somehow looked warm and friendly. Though night blanketed the valley, lights shone from clusters of homes sprinkled throughout—and I recalled gazing from the window of the seraglio at a manse where we'd stopped for the night on my wedding journey. I'd been dreamy, doped up on opos for the pain and to make me docile, but I'd wondered about people living beyond those glowing windows, trying to imagine another life besides my own.

I'd never lost that curiosity—but I had seen inside many windows since, and I'd learned that lives could be lived in thousands of ways, some in contentment, some not. A light inside didn't necessarily mean anything. Still, I smiled wistfully to see them, remembering my first inkling that there could be something more to life than what I'd had at the time.

Zynda landed in a lightless field, while Kiraka circled high above. We'd all agreed the sight of Kral's recently exiled self wouldn't reassure anyone—and even he had seen the humor in that potential confrontation. Zynda slid flat onto her stomach in the grass, wings folded. Marskal looked over his shoulder at me. "Zynda says your arms are getting sore from all the climbing, and that's she's sorry, but this is the best she can do, short of dumping you off—which we think would hurt more."

"Thank you, Zynda," I said quietly, knowing she'd hear me. I shimmied down the ladder, waiting for Harlan. "Your shoulders aren't sore?" I asked.

He grinned at me. "I work out a lot."

"I do, too," I grumbled. Just apparently not like that. "I bet my legs are stronger than yours."

"With that deep-knee work you can do? No bet," he replied amiably. "I'm happy to yield the point."

We jogged across the darkened meadow. Guards would be coming to investigate the great *thing* that had landed, and we preferred to have that conversation at a good distance from Zynda herself. Harlan drew his broadsword, standing just before me and to my left, while I held my own sword in my right hand. "That's far enough," Harlan barked in Dasnarian command language, almost startling me, he sounded so much like the brutal guards I'd hated. He glanced at me and winked, and I relaxed a little.

Using my most regal tone of command, I called out, "Inform Prince Fredrick and Princessa Adaladja that Her Highness Imperial Princess Jenna has come to pay them a visit." I nearly apologized for waking them in the middle of the night, but that would be out of character.

The men had halted, and their leader stilled in confusion. Their discipline was good, however, because he dispatched a man to carry the message, then held his ground. "Apologies for the lack of courtesy, Your Imperial Highness," he said, not bowing or taking his eyes off of us, "as we wait for instruction."

We waited, and I used meditative breathing to keep from pacing nervously. If they refused to come, or if they didn't believe the message and gave orders for us to be repelled—or did believe and nobly sought to rid the empire of a pair of exiled rebel Konyngrrs—we'd be in for trouble.

A turmoil at the castle gates, then a figure running over the lit drawbridge, colorful silks streaming. She barreled toward us, skidding to a halt on bare feet. Princessa Adaladja, a little older—like I was—but very much as she'd looked all those years ago. "Jenna," she breathed, then launched herself at me, heedless of my naked sword.

She embraced me in a fierce hug, chanting my name, then pulled back to frame my face in her hands. "It *is* you! I just knew you'd escaped. I never once believed those stories that you'd died. *Look* at you! See, Fredrick," she called to the approaching prince. "I told you she got away—and that she'd return in triumph."

"I'm not certain that appearing in a darkened meadow in Robsyn counts as triumph, Ada sweetheart," he remarked dryly as he approached, his hair entirely silver now, instead of threaded with it, as it had been back then, "but we welcome you, Your Imperial Highness. I think," he added, making a question of it—and looking Harlan over, not recognizing him, but no doubt catching the family resemblance.

"I completely understand your hesitation," I said, "and if you prefer we leave without troubling you further, we will."

"You will not," Ada said fiercely, clutching my arms as if she'd bodily prevent me from going. "I couldn't help you then, Your Imperial Highness, but you wouldn't be here now if you weren't ready to ask for it."

"Thank you." I took her hands and gripped them, speaking with all the fervency of words waiting to be spoken for decades. "You were the first and almost only person to offer me help. I didn't thank you then. I hope you understand that I wasn't capable of it, but you offering that help started my feet on a path to freedom."

Tears brightened her eyes in the flickering light of the torches their escort carried. "I'm so glad, Your Imperial Highness."

"No title, not anymore." I smiled at her and Fredrick. "I go by the name Ivariel now, and this is my brother, Harlan."

Fredrick jerked, staring at Harlan again. "Harlan Konyngrr. Also missing these last two decades. The eldest and the youngest of old Einarr's legitimate heirs, long exiled, and now returned." He shook his head. "Thus begin the end times."

"Oh, don't be so superstitious, Freddie," Ada said. "We welcome you also, Harlan. Won't you both come in? We'll rouse the kitchens to feed you, then you can sleep." She peered past me into the darkness. "Along with your entourage, if you have one. Do you have horses?"

"It's a very long story, but no. And we cannot linger. If possible, however, could I purchase three klúts from you, along with suitable accessories?"

She blinked at me, completely taken aback. Oh right—I shouldn't be handling money at all, nor should I be offering to buy what my rank as part of the imperial family entitled me to take. "Of course I can *give* you several klúts, and appropriate jewelry," she replied, recovering admirably.

"Suitable for the Imperial Palace," I told her. We had to be able to blend in for at least a short time.

"Not a problem." She beckoned to a younger man and sent him running back across the moat bridge.

"Other than that," I continued, "all we ask is the use of your meadow for the night—and your discretion."

"Of course, we—" Ada began.

"Discretion can be interpreted as treachery, depending on whose secrets one is keeping," Fredrick put in, laying an admonishing hand on Ada's shoulder. "Giving clothes to passing strangers is one thing. I cannot in good conscience blindly agree to something that might put Robsyn and our people at risk," he told her more gently. "We have responsibilities to our kingdom as well."

"I understand." I briefly debated how much to tell them. "We intend to depose Hestar," I said baldly. Harlan didn't flinch, but his eyes caught the light as he glanced at me. Yes, I wasn't sure this was a good idea either. But they wouldn't be able to send a message to the Imperial Palace faster than we could fly there, and if we didn't succeed tonight, then we'd either be dead or have to develop another plan anyway.

Ada had clasped her hands together, watching Fredrick with hope in her face. He looked more agonized than anything. Fisting his hands on his hips, he stared at the ground for several long moments, then let out a long sigh. "The end times, indeed."

"Hestar has been aggressively attacking other realms," Harlan put in gravely. "And he is corrupt. He and the dowager empress have been trafficking with the Temple of Deyrr to consolidate and extend their power. We don't wish to end the empire, only the authoritarian tyranny that is rotting its core."

"Deyrr." Fredrick growled the name, watch Harlan somberly, thinking hard, while Ada shot him a sorrowful look. "Then the rumors are true," he said quietly, flicking a glance at his wife. "And, yes, I know you said so."

"I didn't want it to be true," she told him, laying a hand on his arm. "You're so good that it's hard for you to imagine evil in others."

"A pretty compliment," he said, but without rancor, covering her hand with his. "I have taken oaths of loyalty to the emperor, however. I cannot aid you in this, no matter how I might feel personally."

And there it was. We'd have to find another landing spot. "I understand. I wouldn't ask you to betray an oath."

"Your oaths would include stopping us," Harlan pointed out, "now that you are aware of our plan."

Fredrick gave him a narrow smile. "Am I? I don't see how I could know anything. Nobody goes in that meadow at night," he added, raising his voice to the small group of guards and retainers. "I appreciate your vigilance in calling us out here. No fault of yours that it was a false alarm. You can all return to your duties with easy minds, knowing we saw and heard nothing."

"Sir!" The men shouted as one, saluting.

"You are a good man, Fredrick." Ada kissed him on the cheek, then turned to embrace me once more. "Good luck," she whispered. "I know you'll succeed. And afterward, perhaps we can be friends."

"We always have been." I hugged her back, then bowed to Fredrick. "Thank you, Prince Fredrick. You are a good man, and a good ruler. And a good husband," I added. "Hearing that Ada loved and trusted you, so long ago—that was the first time I understood that such marriages were possible. If it's in my power to reward you, I will."

A young woman dashed out of the castle, barefoot and carrying a satchel. She gave it to Ada, who quickly checked the contents, then handed it to me. "I wish I could do more."

"You've done what was needed, and that's everything."

Harlan bowed, too, then shook Fredrick's hand. "I offer my thanks also—and hope for fruitful future alliances."

We walked back into the moonless night to where Zynda and Marskal waited, and told Zynda to give the go ahead for Kiraka to land.

~ 12 ~

"I NEVER THOUGHT I'd have to put on one of these things again," Jepp groused, "unless for sex play, anyway. And then I just kind of drape it on long enough for Kral to take off again."

"They're not so bad," Karyn commented. "Hold still, though."

"I have my outfit from before, you know, back on the *Hákyrling*," Jepp continued. "Inga and Helva had it made for me. I could fight in that. I still don't see why I couldn't wear it."

"Because everyone remembers it," Karyn replied patiently. "You stand out enough as it is. And if you'd hold still for three breaths instead of bitching, I would've been done already."

"I liked you better when you were all humble and apologetic," Jepp replied.

"No you didn't." Karyn sounded amused and not at all offended. Their voices drifted to me from a short distance away. The guys had convened in a circle lit by the glow of Zynda's and Kiraka's eyes, consulting on their plans and giving us the privacy of darkness to change into the klúts Ada had given us. I couldn't see the color, but the fine texture of the embroidered silk revealed their rich quality—and snagged on my hands, no longer those of a lady of leisure, but callused from years of working with harness and weapons.

Once I'd had an entire room devoted to my klúts, the finest an empire could provide for their priceless pearl. "I never thought to don one again either," I said, then swallowed my pride. "And I'm afraid I need help, too, Karyn."

"Be right there," she replied.

"Been over twenty years, huh?" Jepp commented. "Enough time to forget old habits."

A good excuse she offered me, but... "I'm chagrined to confess I never dressed myself," I said. "I thought maybe I could remember, but it's not working out."

"Seriously?" Jepp sounded incredulous. "I know you were pampered and all, but who doesn't know how to dress herself?"

"An imperial princess," Karyn answered her sharply. "Don't be so judgmental."

"I'm not! I'm really not, Ivariel." She sounded stricken.

"It's all right," I reassured her. Karyn came to me and took the long banner of silk from my hands, sorting its folds by feel. "I *was* pampered, and beyond ignorant. When I escaped, I wore men's clothes that Harlan had acquired. They hung off me, and—because of them and because I'd cut my hair off short—I thought I looked like a boy."

"I'll have to touch you," Karyn said, silently voicing my title, asking permission, and apologizing all at once.

"That's fine," I replied mildly. It felt odd to stand naked in the darkness—one wears nothing under a klút—as Karyn wound the silk firmly around my waist and hips, then over my rib cage and bosom, before adding the looser, more elaborate outer folds. The sensation took me back viscerally to that girl I'd been, the thousands of times I'd stood placidly while my servant girls dressed me in lengths of silk I'd wear for maybe a day and never again. I hadn't had any idea what went into weaving that material, the careful cultivation of the silk worms, and the countless hours of painstaking work to make thread and then fabric. And that was before the embroidering.

I'd gone through in a few hours the product of a year of another woman's life and thought nothing of it. Since then, I'd learned. Much as Ochieng complained about the rainy season, that's when we'd spend our days indoors, when Zalaika and Ochieng's sisters and brothers had taught me the skills necessary to our lives. I'd learned to spin thread and to weave, as well as to carve wood, both for necessities and to make art. My son and daughters had grown up learning those things, too—and they'd grown up together. I'd been fiercely glad to see my daughters riding elephants and learning to fight alongside my son.

And yet, somewhere along the way I'd forgotten, too. Forgotten about the suffocating silk and life of enforced indolence that led to petty selfishness. I'd spared them that, if nothing else.

"There," Karyn said, patting the last fold into place to drape over my shoulder. "Though you should probably take your hair down," she added hesitantly. "I have a comb—I can do it for you. I'm taking mine down."

"Good idea." We walked back to the circle of light. Of course I'd have to take down my braids. The style would look far too foreign. But it also gave me a pang. Kajala had done the braiding for me, interweaving the obsidian and copper jewelry I'd acquired over the years.

We stepped into the light and all four men looked up. Kral eyed Jepp with a decidedly lustful glint and she pointed a finger at him. "Don't start with me. We don't have time and I'm still mad at you."

Sorting through the jewelry, we added ear bangles, necklaces, anklets and arm bands.

"With your permission?" Karyn asked, holding the comb, and I nodded. She began extracting my Nyamburan hair jewelry, placing the pieces in my cupped palms, unraveling the braids. Harlan watched with an odd expression, as I exchanged my Nyamburan self for the Dasnarian one. Jenna coming ever nearer to the surface.

"I hadn't seen the traditional Dasnarian garb for women before," Marskal commented. "They're quite beautiful."

"Dasnarian women are committed to being decorative," I commented in a wry tone and Karyn snorted softly. She combed out the last of my braids, and I went to Harlan, holding out the hair jewelry. "Would you keep these for me? I don't have pockets now."

He accepted the handful gravely, eyes never straying from me as he stowed them in a bag on his belt. "You look…" His voice broke off and he didn't finish. Clearing his throat, he said he needed a moment, and strode off into the darkness.

Bemused, I turned to find Kral staring after Harlan's back. Transferring his gaze to me, he smiled sadly. "You look very much like you did, back then. With your hair down and in that color." He gestured vaguely.

Looking down, I realized that, by some fluke of hlyti, I wore a pale color, possibly ivory or white. They'd dressed me in exclusively those shades for my wedding festivities, to emphasize my pale skin and notable hair. And I'd worn diamonds and pearls. My stomach turned and I wondered if I needed a moment alone in the night, too.

"I'll talk to him," Kral said, following after Harlan, so I stayed where I was.

"Here," Jepp said, bringing over some leather straps. "I've got some thigh sheaths you can borrow. They don't show under the klút, if you're careful."

She helped me strap them on, showing me how to secure them. I sheathed my blades, practicing the draw. As we did,

Karyn went to Zyr and turned her back. He untied the ribbon holding her braid, then held it out to her. With a smile more intimate than seemed relevant to the gesture, she tied the ribbon around his wrist, then handed him the comb. His expression reverent, he combed out her hair, speaking quietly enough that I couldn't hear, but her blush gave the content away.

"I'd like to find a place for this one," Jepp commented, casually twirling a heftier blade than her usual paired daggers, "but it's too big to conceal. Guess I'll have to give it to Kral to hold for me. *Again.*"

She sounded so aggrieved that I paused in practicing with my blades to look at the one she fussed with, then froze. "Where did you get that?" I demanded, the black red of Jenna's rising inner demon edging around my vision. The red rage Harlan had called it.

Jepp eyed me warily, a bit indignant. "It was my mother's."

Oh. Oh, right. Of course it wasn't the same blade. It made sense that Kaja had more than one like it. I needed to get a grip. The past kept overtaking the present in unexpected ways.

"Seen a ghost?" Jepp asked, not without sympathy. "Mom probably had it with her when you knew her. Kaedrin brought it to me after Mom died."

"Kaja had at least two of them," I said, feeling a bit calmer. Jepp had a steadying influence with her practicality, not unlike her mother. "Because Kaedrin sent one just like this to me also, after Kaja died, with a message from Kaja that I should plant it where it belonged."

Jepp frowned, spinning the blade thoughtfully. "Cryptic. Did you know what she meant?"

I laughed without humor. "I did. And when my late ex-husband came after me, I planted it in his heart. So far as I know, it lies there still."

"Good girl," Jepp murmured. "And that would've creeped me out too. But the dead don't rise to haunt us, no matter what the stories claim. Unless Deyrr animated them," she added. "Also creepy."

"Fortunately Deyrr is done for."

"Yeah." She grimaced. "Now we only have living monsters to deal with."

"By dawn they might also be done for."

"Your mouth to Danu's ear. My hand to Danu's blade," Jepp affirmed.

"All right, soldiers," Kral declared as he and Harlan emerged from the shadows. "Time to get aloft."

"Are you sure you want to carry me?" Marskal asked Zyr. "Zynda says that Kiraka can handle all three of us."

"Yes, yes, mossback," Zyr sneered with a wave of his hand at Marskal's lanky frame. "I'm rested, this is the plan, and you don't weigh much more than Karyn does. Why—afraid I'll drop you?"

"I did beat you in that last match of I Eat You," Marskal said with such blandness that I'd have thought nothing of it, if Zyr hadn't glowered.

"You cheated," he growled.

"Using a blade against claws isn't cheating. It's evening the odds," Marskal replied. Zynda blew smoke over him, lowering her head, and he laughed, leaning against her snout and stroking it. Kral was similarly saying goodbye to Jepp in a far more lusty fashion—she apparently wasn't *that* mad—and Karyn and Zyr embraced, sharing a long kiss.

Harlan and I looked at each other, somewhat bemused. "Our fault for ditching our own spouses, I suppose," he commented.

"Ursula didn't sound annoyed," I replied, "so far as I could tell."

"No, she didn't to me either. Worried though. As Ochieng sounded. So far as I could tell," he added with a smile.

Yes, hearing tone via Jepp via Andi hadn't been easy. "We'll just have to return safely so they can fret over us—and so we can make it up to them."

"Good plan." He gave me a penetrating look. "Speaking of, are you doing all right?"

"Are *you*?" I shot back.

He shook his head slowly, not negating, but thoughtfully. "It's a helluva thing, isn't it, us going back there. Into the lions' den. On purpose."

"Yes." I pressed my hand to my fluttering belly. "I keep thinking I smell jasmine."

"Maybe it's the klút?"

I lifted a fold from my shoulder and sniffed it. "Oh, Danu take me. Yes. Glad to know I'm not crazy. Not in that way, anyhow."

"When you go inside the palace…" He hesitated, searching for words. "You might remember things."

"Believe me, Harlan, I've never been able to forget."

He inclined his chin somberly. "No doubt. I know you can do this," he said with such grave confidence I knew he meant it.

"I can," I agreed. "And it occurs to me, that *we* are the lions now. They have no idea we're coming after them. They think they're safe, but they aren't. They've owed us a debt for a very long time, and it's accrued a great deal of interest."

He grinned, a bloodthirsty quality to it. "Time for them to pay up."

Yes. Yes, it was more than time.

~ 13 ~

KARYN HAD THE most experience flying, so she sat in front, and Jepp insisted on rear guard, so I ended up in the middle again—sandwiched between silk-clad, curved bodies this time. Zynda stayed low, so we wouldn't get too cold, but the wind blew chill enough for me to be glad of their warmth. Jepp slid an arm around my waist and sniffed my neck. "You smell good."

"It's the klút," I informed her.

"No, I think it's you." Her breath whuffed over my skin. "Can I taste?"

"You may not," I replied firmly.

"You ever try a woman?" she asked.

"I've only ever been with Ochieng," I replied.

"Only one lover, in your *whole life?*" She made it sound like I'd told her I'd only ever eaten bread and water.

"Well, there was my horrible late ex-husband," I said, "but I don't count him."

"No, he absolutely doesn't count." She was quiet a moment. "Still, only one lover ever, and a guy. Maybe Ochieng would be open to mixing it up. He's super hot, too."

I had to laugh. "I thought you were monogamous with Kral."

"Yeah." She was trying to sound glum about it, but I could

tell she didn't mind. "But fantasies and flirting are still totally fine. It's good to think about fun life things, you know?"

I did understand that. When Zynda's wings stopped their steady pumping and she went into a silent glide, I knew we must be approaching the Imperial Palace. Craning my neck to see, I soon spotted it. Though I'd only seen my home of eighteen years from the outside that once, the image had seared itself into my memory.

It looked much the same, though smaller from our height. The mirror-still lake surrounding the edifice reflected the towers, walls, and turrets—all brightly lit with torches and fire pits— making it into a kind of star that had points going down as well as up. The sheer polished stone looked cold even in full summer, and the barren perimeter all around the lake was a sterile expanse of black, surrounded by the deeper dark of the thick forest.

I also saw what I hadn't had the wit or experience to note before. Guard stations dotted the lakeshore—facing out, from what the others had reported—and supposedly another set just within the forest boundary faced in. I couldn't see those in the impenetrable night, but the soldiers on the torchlit walls stood out clearly. So Dasnarian in their precise spacing and rigid postures, their black beetle armor shining with firelight.

Karyn strung her bow, then drew a few arrows from her quiver, and laid them against her thigh. We planned on stealth, but prepared for the worst.

"All right, Andi," Jepp muttered. "You see? Good. Tell Zynda to make a pass so I can pick my tower."

Zynda obediently angled to circle. I held my breath, as if that would keep the soldiers manning the walls from spotting us. We were losing altitude on the glide, and I kept feeling like I wanted to flap my arms or something to pull us higher.

We made a full circle of the Imperial Palace, Jepp muttering to herself—or to Andi—and I finally began to assimilate just how huge the complex was. The seraglio had been large enough to comfortably hold several hundred women, but I'd never quite framed my mind around how much larger the rest of the Imperial Palace must be. It was like a city, condensed and piled on top of itself behind sheer walls.

"Ask Zynda for one more pass," Jepp murmured, "if she can do it without flapping. It was definitely one of the towers on the far side."

"We're so low," I whispered.

"I may have excellent long sight," Jepp replied quietly in my ear, "but even I need to be closer to pick out the exact unlit window I want. And we want to be sure, because she's going to have to flap her wings to hover long enough for us to drop onto the top."

I began to wonder why this plan had sounded good. It was a terrible plan. So risky, so much that could go wrong.

Zynda glided around, and we all held still. It seemed impossible that the guards didn't look up, didn't sense the enormous dark shadow blacking out the stars as she circled overhead.

"That's the one." Jepp pointed, sighting along her arm, Karyn leaning back to get the right angle. "Got it?"

"Two archers atop," Karyn said quietly. "One is easy. Two is a problem."

"Drop me first and I'll kill the second."

"All right."

"No," I said. "We need Jepp to talk to Zynda and Andi. I'll do the drop."

"You'll have to hang from the rope. Might be a high fall, hard bounce—then you'd have to react fast."

"I can do it."

"Get ready then. Remember: land lightly, knees flexed.

Bounce."

"I've got it, Jepp," I replied. Definitely Kaja's daughter.

She chuckled. "Kill the lights, Andi."

It felt like when a dust storm suddenly blows in—or like when the magic barrier moved—scraping over my senses and making my ears pop. The air compressed, then expanded, and all the torches and pit fires winked out, leaving us in blackness.

Zynda dipped a wing sharply, pivoting on the point and angling us nearly sideways. I yipped in alarm, holding onto the rope harness in a desperate grip.

"Steady," Jepp murmured. "Like dancing with a partner, go with her lead."

"Like you ever let anyone lead," I muttered back and she laughed softly.

Karyn raised her bow, the arrow placed against the string, but hanging without tension. "I can't see a thing," she said. "Zynda is going to have to point me."

"Over her left shoulder. On my mark," Jepp replied. "Ivariel, get in position. I'll count down."

I drew a small dagger and clenched it in my teeth. Not an ideal maneuver and Kaja would've had sharp words for me, but I needed both hands to climb. Carefully shimmying down Zynda's side, I told myself it was like doing tricks with Efe as she galloped and tried to shake me off. I wasn't hanging in midair off the side of dragon, poised to plummet to my death. No, no—because that would be foolish and risky.

"Three," came Jepp's soft count.

We dropped, angled into a tight spiral, I clung like a burr, deciding it would be a good time to pray to Danu for assistance.

"Two."

Zynda leveled out, going in for a straight glide. The shouts of men drifted up, and I could barely make out the black silhouette of the tower. I'd reached the bottom of the ladder, watching the rapid approach of the looming tower, bitterly regretting that I'd impulsively volunteered. This would be a dicey move even if I'd practiced it a hundred times. What in Danu had I been thinking?

"And...." Came Jepp's soft warning. "One!"

Zynda swung her head and the tower lit with the blue glow. One guard yelped. The other already crumpling with Karyn's arrow through his throat. Zynda backwinged. The rope swung.

I let go. *Bounce*, I told myself.

The impact thudded up through my ankles and knees—but I was on the tower!—and my strong dancer's legs held, serving me well as they always had. The guard gaped at the impossible sight of me: a klút-clad, bejweled woman dropping out of the sky. He recovered and charged me. I spun, cutting his throat, and then crouched, waiting for an alarm to be sounded.

Lots of shouting, but it sounded disorganized. I sorted the Dasnarian military commands, not hearing any indication of orders sending guards to my tower. Sneaking up to a crenellation, I peered over the edge. Darkness and chaos. Then a blaze of light.

Kral, fully armored, stepped out onto the barren periphery between lake and forest, Harlan a step beside and behind him. "Hestar!" Kral bellowed, his strong male voice carrying over the water and cutting through the shouts of soldiers, silencing them. "I challenge you for right to the throne of the Dasnarian Empire. Show yourself, you cowardly worm!"

Well, fuck me. That had not been in the plans. Not the ones they told us about.

A whoosh of wind had me looking up, just as an immense black shadow moved to block the stars, the beat of Zynda's wings as she hovered whipping my loose hair around my face.—

and Jepp dropped lightly beside. "Good bounce," she said. "But what in Danu's freezing tits does that lunkhead think he's doing?"

"Hestar!" Krall bellowed again. "I claim the *bjoja at haseti.* Fight or yield!"

"The boh-jah thing again, more recompense?" Jepp asked with exasperation.

"That was *at satt.* This is *at haseti*—a challenge of honor for the right to rule," I explained. "As a legitimate son of the previous emperor, Kral can challenge Hestar's for the throne. Single combat."

Jepp cursed foully, then stood to grab the dangling rope ladder and steady it for Karyn's climb down. "Did you know about this?" she demanded in a hush, when Karyn dropped beside us.

"No, but I'm not surprised," she replied. "It *is* an excellent distraction, you have to admit."

"I admit no such thing," Jepp snarled. "Can he win?"

"I don't know," I confessed.

"It's not something women would know," Karyn added quietly. "I know he had many reasons not to try it before."

Jepp cursed again. "Why do I even ask? I'm fucked either way."

As my eyes adapted to the dark—and as the watchfires were relit, I realized—I could see she was rigging up a rope to the crenellation. "If that Dasnarian brute thinks he's going to stick me in this Danu-forsaken place, prancing about in silks and jewels—no offense—he's even thicker-skulled than I thought," she muttered. "Cover me."

Karyn nocked an arrow and edged up to the parapet as Jepp dropped over the side. Hoarse shouts echoed up from below, the palace stirring as orders were relayed. "She's in," Karyn told me. "Your turn."

I sheathed my blade and crawled over the edge, shimmying down the rope. At least it wasn't swinging from a dragon. My shoulders were going to ache for weeks, however. If I lived through this. Firm hands gripped my hips, pulling me toward a window ledge, and I felt with my feet for leverage.

"I've got you," Jepp whispered. "Let go."

I released the rope, sinking my weight so I wouldn't overbalance, and Jepp helped me step into the room. "You're a natural," she said, giving me an approving pat. "Come down, Karyn."

The room was even darker than the night outside, and I waited, smoothing my hair and checking the folds of my klút— then sighed as I met with a stiffening wet spot. Blood, no doubt. So much for blending in with my fancy borrowed outfit. Jepp pulled Karyn in with a muffled thud as they both fell to the floor.

"Sorry, sorry," Karyn muttered, and Jepp snorted.

"If you wanted to get me on my back, then—"

"Jepp!" Karyn cut her off, sounding aghast. I'd found the curtains hung by the window and pulled them across, then felt around for a candle I knew must be nearby. There it was, and a flint striker conveniently close. It took me a couple of tries, but I got the candle lit. Pleased with myself, I glanced around the room...

Inside me, Jenna wailed in terror. In this room—or one just like it—I'd been strung up naked, blood running down my arms where the marriage manacles cut into my young skin. And Rodolf, he...

He...

A red-black wave welled up and swamped me. Like the river at Nyambura at full flood stage, it tumbled me like a piece of kindling, dragging me under to drown.

~ 14 ~

"**B**REATHE." JEPP'S VOICE came from a far distance. "Breathe, Ivariel. In and out, nice and steady. You're safe. I've got you. Just breathe."

"Here, it's as cold as I can manage," Karyn said.

A cool, damp cloth wrapped the back of my neck. I was kneeling on the thick carpet, my head held firmly down by Jepp's practiced hand as she stroked my back with the other. "That's it, honey," she crooned. "Even breaths. You're safe. All is well."

I opened my eyes, taking in the elaborate Dasnarian design of the plush carpet. "I've invaded the Imperial Palace and am hiding from the guards of a brother who'd kill me on sight. Or worse," I commented drily. "I think safe is the wrong word."

Jepp released my head with a chuckle of relief. "And she's back. Nothing wrong with the good sense Danu gave you."

I sat up slowly, aware of the distant rushing in my ears. Karyn stood by the door, holding a dagger. She'd had to leave the too-obvious bow and quiver on top of the tower. She gave me an anxious look. "What happened?"

Feeling as if I'd been stepped on by an elephant—and even if they don't mean to do it, it's crushing like you wouldn't believe—I scrubbed my hands over my face. "Bad memories."

"I thought you didn't leave the seraglio," Jepp said.

"Except after my wedding, when I was summoned to serve

my husband, in a room very like this one." If not this exact one. Probably they were all pretty much the same though.

"Shit, Ivariel." Jepp looked horrified, her face pale and eyes huge and dark in it. "I didn't think."

"I didn't either." Though Harlan had warned me. At least crazed Jenna had receded quickly and left me in rational control again. I got to my feet, carefully not looking around. "What's happened?"

"Lots of commotion, but we can't see the duel from here." Jepp looked thoroughly annoyed, which at least brought the snap back to her eyes.

A fist pounded on the door and we all jumped. Karyn flattened herself beside it. Jepp and I drew our blades. "All women back to the seraglio!" a male voice shouted, then moved to hammer on the next door down.

Jepp looked to me and Karyn. "Recalling the women to safety?" she asked.

We nodded and she grinned. "That works into our plan just fine. When a group of women goes by, we'll join up in the parade and head meekly to the seraglio. Except I don't know what we're going to do about the blood on Ivariel's klút."

I looked down at the well-spattered ivory silk, the blood drying to brown in the smaller spots, but still brightly crimson in the biggest, and dampest, circle. Karyn grimaced, giving me a wary look. "Not to incite any more bad memories, but she wouldn't be the first woman to return from a night of bed sport with blood on her klút. Her own."

She was right, I realized. All those nights I staggered—or was carried—back to the dubious safety of the seraglio after Rodolf was done with me, I'd been battered and bloody. No one had blinked an eye. "Fortunately I know how to play that role," I commented.

"If you say so." Jepp looked appalled, but nodded crisply, then went to the door to ease it open. "Here comes a group, let's slide in behind them." She drew a loose fold of her klút over her head to hide her short hair. Karyn handed her a thin shawl of silk to cover her brown skinned bare arms, which would excite notice. Jepp peeked out the door again, glanced back at me. "Showtime," she whispered.

We shuffled out the door behind her. Karyn transformed into a meek and submissive Dasnarian woman, graceful with her demurely lowered gaze. "Stop swaggering," she hissed at Jepp. "And look down."

I kept a hand clasped to my face on the side with the most blood, recalling how my body had felt so weak, so broken. After that rush of overwhelming memory, poor newlywed Jenna lurked close under my skin, and it didn't take much to summon the proper demeanor. The tears rose up and I let them fall, partly in homage for that girl who'd shed a thousand tears when no one had cared. They'd wanted my obedience and hadn't cared what it cost me.

Jenna and I would shed our tears. And then we would exact payment for them.

The thick carpets on my bare feet were the same, as were the guards stationed along the hall. They commented on the charms of the women who passed, the lewd references understandable to me now as they hadn't been then.

And, as if shedding those tears released the last of that dragging grief for all my shattered dreams, the anger began to sizzle in my belly. I stoked it, feeding that fire with all the righteous fuel it required. The women around me—wives, concubines, and rekjabrel alike—murmured amongst themselves as the guards herded us down the hallway. Some had heard the commotion. Others had been with men who'd hastily thrown on armor and grabbed weapons.

Hestar was going out to the challenger, a richly clad woman near us was saying. Who was it? It couldn't be Kral because... the woman speaking slowed so I nearly bumped into her. She cast a sharp, sideways glance at Karyn, then did a double take.

Uh oh.

"Maybe it *is* Kral," she said significantly. "Karyn af Hardie— is that you? We thought you were dead." Her silver laugh tinkled brightly.

Jepp had a silver dagger at the woman's ribs, looping her other arm companionably around her. "There, there," she said in very rough Dasnarian—and male command language. "Poor thing is confused. Too much opos smoke will mess up your brain."

The woman stiffened, but walked on compliantly enough in Jepp's unyielding grip. Fortunately we soon reached the staircase where the male guards were required to remain and we descended, a river of silk-clad women, gazes lifting and voices rising now that they no longer need be so meek.

Jepp kept hold of the woman, someone I didn't recognize, and marched her along, chattering cheerfully in her ear about the technique for gutting a deer. The woman looked faint and occasionally stumbled, but Jepp didn't let her fall.

"She terrified me, too, the first time I met her," Karyn confided. "Now I know she's actually soft-hearted—even sweet— under that brash attitude. She flirts more when she's nervous."

I'd dropped my hand, no longer needing to playact for the guards and wryly acknowledged Karyn's observation. "She and Kral might be perfect for each other."

"Didn't take me long to figure that out either," Karyn admitted.

"Sorry," I said, belatedly remembering Kral had been Karyn's husband at the time. "That was thoughtless of me."

"Not at all," she replied with a smile. "I never loved him. I wasn't even alive back then. If not for Jepp, I would've stayed that way and I might never have found Zyr. Funny how *hlyti* has guided our feet."

Indeed. We reached the bottom of the stairs, the women edging into singles and pairs as they filed through the great brass-and-wood doors that would seal the seraglio. So many memories of those doors—almost all of them from the other side—as I watched the boys leave and never come back, the concubines, rekjabrel and wives going as they were summoned.

The few times I'd passed through those doors, how I'd felt coming back, and how I'd screamed and begged not to be sent through again. Hede, the seraglio enforcer, with her whip, hard hands, and unswerving commitment to the rules still featured in my nightmares. She'd been the one to flog me when I was a child, albeit at my mother's command, and it had been Hede who tied me to a litter with casual brutality, so I could be carried back for another night of marital torture.

A trickle of cold sweat ran down between my breasts, and I said a prayer to Danu to clear my mind. That was the past. The past couldn't hurt me.

I am the lion now.

But I braced myself for the sight of Hede. It could be that she'd since died. She'd seemed old to me then, but probably she hadn't been much older than my mother. Besides, the cruel mistress of the whip had always seemed too tough to die.

But it was a different female guard who stood to one side, a coiled whip hanging from the belt cinching her klút to her waist.

Jepp's captive edged toward the guard, opened her mouth, then squeaked as Jepp poked her with the blade and pushed her firmly through the doors.

"You won't get away with this," Jepp's captive hissed. "My husband is His Imperial Highness Prince Leo and—"

Jepp shut her up with a hard yank of the woman's hair. As soon as we passed the guard, I reached back, pulled Leo's wife through the doorway and into a thick stand of ferns, pinning the struggling woman against a palm tree that had stood there since I was a girl.

Like I said, Dasnaria is not a place of rapid change. Or, really, much change at all.

Covering the woman's mouth, I stared into her eyes. "You will be silent," I commanded with imperial iciness. "For I am Her Imperial Highness Princess Jenna, and I outrank your ass."

The woman's eyes widened—in shock, disbelief, or the urge to kill, I didn't know—then a voice I hadn't heard in over twenty years spoke behind me.

"Jenna?"

~ 15 ~

I RELEASED MY cowed prey and spun. Inga.

For a moment, I experienced that weird double vision, the disorienting overlap of past and present. Inga at seventeen and Inga over twenty years later. The same, so much the same. Her hair gleamed in the same golden curls, and she was still so lovely with those extraordinary aqua eyes—and also sharper, honed, with a weary wisdom in place of the starry enthusiasm that had once shone in those eyes. And she carried herself like an empress.

Had it been the same for Harlan, seeing me again? I thought maybe so.

"Inga," I breathed. And then we were in each others arms, weeping and laughing at once.

"Get Helva," Inga called over my shoulder. "Fast as you can. Hurry!"

"What is the meaning of this?" Leo's wife tried to pull us apart. "I'm reporting this to—"

"One word," Inga said with slicing authority, a blade of reprimand, even as she held on to me. "You speak *one word* without my permission, Jasmyra, and I will crush you."

"You can't run my life, Inga," Jasmyra hissed, glaring at me. "I don't know who you are, but everyone knows Jenna is dead. I'm informing the Dowager Empress."

"Don't you—" Inga began, but I stopped her.

"Please do," I said pleasantly. "In fact, you may inform my mother she can expect to receive me in a few moments." I was keeping an eye on the door—as were Karyn and Jepp—and the flow of women had slowed to a trickle. Soon they'd close and bar the doors, keeping us safe while the men battled. Sealing us in until someone let us out again.

A shriek echoed across the lagoon, making me whip my head around, blade in hand. Jepp had pulled a blade, too—then quickly vanished it into a fold of her klút, giving me a sheepish smile. A lean arrow of a woman streaked around the manmade lake, her klút hiked up around her knees as she ran, dark blond hair streaming behind her.

Helva launched herself at me, and I caught her with the strength of years of resisting being toppled by a mischievous elephant. "I knew you'd come back for us. I *knew*! Didn't I tell you, Inga? Didn't I!"

"You did," Inga agreed with a soft smile, then looked at me. "Helva never doubted."

"But you did," I replied, seeing it in her face.

"Inga is the *practical* one." Helva said it like an insult, releasing me and wiping her tears.

Inga tipped her head in rueful acknowledgment. "It *has* been a long time," she pointed out. "First Harlan never returned, then we do get word of him, but his spy Jepp had never heard of you."

"Scout," Jepp corrected, swaggering over now that the guards had put the bars on the doors. "Hey Inga, Helva—you're both looking exceptionally lovely."

"Well, this is a day," Inga observed, each of them embracing Jepp. Inga looked past her and her eyes widened. "And Karyn, too. All our disappeared are returning, like ghosts drawn back to the tombs of our ancestors."

"That's not a grim analogy or anything," Jepp muttered.

"We Dasnarians are a grim lot," Inga observed, but Helva rolled her eyes and shook her head behind Inga's back. When her sister sent her a suspicious glare, Helva beamed with innocence. It was as if time had stood still in this place, which looked exactly the same as the day I'd left. So much so that I shivered inside—and had to remind myself I could leave anytime.

Well, once someone let us out.

"All of you go about your business," Inga commanded with the cool ease of someone expecting to be obeyed. The lingering women dispersed, dragging their feet at their missed opportunity to eavesdrop on hot gossip, and Inga moved us away from the foliage and into a clearing.

"Dare I ask if anyone else has returned with you?" Inga lowered her voice, and I recalled how there was no privacy in the seraglio. No conversation could be held unheard. This was as close as it got to privacy—being certain no one lingered nearby, or behind the walls.

"Let's call it a family reunion," I replied as quietly, raising my brows.

"Kral is here then." Inga looked at Jepp and Karyn, standing close as sisters. "So, you are both his wives now?"

They looked at each other and laughed. "Jepp is," Karyn explained. "I'm married to another now."

"We're not exactly married," Jepp protested. "Neither are you, for that matter."

"Yes, we are," Karyn replied smugly. "In the Tala way. And once we're done here, Zyr and I will visit my family at the Hardie estates and he'll sign the contracts with my father."

Jepp snorted with laughter. "Poor Zyr."

"He loves me," Karyn replied with dignity, "and he wants me to be married in the tradition of my people as well as his."

I tried to imagine coaxing Ochieng into negotiating and signing contracts with Hestar to confirm our decades-old marriage, and nearly laughed aloud. Ochieng would do it if I asked—and would probably pull it off brilliantly in his smooth, diplomatic style—but I didn't need that from him. Quite the opposite, as I'd moved past allowing any of my brothers to handle my life for me, even Harlan. But I understood Karyn's need to tie that off, especially since she actually liked her family.

That gave me a pang, so I focused on Inga and Helva, still beaming with joy at seeing me. I liked some of my family, too, and those were the people worth paying attention to. "Our other brother is also with us," I told them.

Helva clapped her hands together and jumped with joy, more like a girl than a woman in her mid-thirties. Inga smiled, and urged her to quiet. Then she turned serious eyes on me. "Where are they?"

"The question of the hour," Jepp growled. "The idiots are probably dead by now."

Helva gasped, hands going to her throat as if to hold it back, her warm brown eyes full of alarm. "What?"

"That's probably overstating," I said, shooting Jepp a jaundiced glare.

"Yeah, well, we spies are a grim lot," she snapped back, and I recognized that worry and frustration rode her. She'd much rather be out there, guarding Kral's back, than locked inside with us.

"We won't be here long," I promised, hoping that would be the case.

"Feeling the weight of all that water crushing down, too?" Jepp stared at the ceiling suspiciously. "Gives me the series willies to know we're basically in a stone cage under a big frozen lake."

"It's summertime," Karyn corrected.

Jepp stabbed a finger at her. "How much you want to bet me that water is cold enough to shrivel even your generous tits to nothing?"

Inga and Helva watched with bemused expressions. I glanced around, making sure Inga's edict had kept the area clear. The women had obeyed her, as they once obeyed Hulda. Interesting.

"Listen," I said, catching their attention while Jepp created a distraction, continuing to complain about drowning, "Kral, Harlan, and other friends are outside. They were to create a distraction for us to sneak in here—but then we heard Kral issue the *bjoja at haseti* to Hestar."

They exchanged glances. "That explains the recall and sealing," Inga said, tipping her head at the barred doors.

"Can Kral defeat Hestar?" I asked.

Inga looked thoughtful. "It will be interesting to find out."

"Well, it's more than a philosophical question," I replied with some aggravation.

Inga raised a single brow. "Someone went and got an education."

"I did." She didn't fool me. Inga was no longer ignorant either—and she was being cagey with me. "We're counting on the guys to get us out of here after I deal with my mother."

"I see. So, you're here because you promised us that you'd return, and to take revenge on your mother. Anything else you plan to accomplish before you leave again?" She had an edge to her voice, ice in her pretty eyes.

"Jenna wouldn't leave us again," Helva said staunchly, then studied my face with dawning grief. "Or will you?"

With a wrench, I realized Helva had truly believed I'd come home to stay. Inga, however, watched me with the cool knowledge that I never would. And I wouldn't. I had no desire to be empress. My home was in Nyambura, with Ochieng, and my family—human and elephant. The knowledge came as a relief, a release of tension I hadn't realized was knotting me up from the inside out. The certainty came so suddenly and clearly that I wondered if Danu had a hand in it.

"I cannot stay. My home is elsewhere now," I told Helva. "I have a husband, children. You could come with me."

"Leave Dasnaria?" Helva made it sound like I'd suggested we fly to the moon. "But—"

"We can discuss all of that later," Inga interrupted smoothly, putting an arm around Helva's waist and drawing her away from me, as if to protect her. "What else, Jenna? There's more. I see it in your face."

"Ivariel," I told her. "I changed my name when I went into hiding, and it's how I think of myself now."

"You are always Jenna to us," she replied with certainty. "There is no shame in being who you were. At least Jenna was a sister to me."

Those words struck my heart, and I remembered the day I said goodbye to them. "I meant to come back long before now," I said, my voice hoarse with old tears. "But the years slipped away."

"Why would you want to come back to this?" she replied, stiffly, but not unkind. "I didn't expect you to come back. I know what this place did to you. But you might have sent a letter."

"I... didn't think you could read," I said, feeling wretched as the words came out of my mouth.

Inga raised a pale brow. "You're not the only one who spent

these last decades enriching herself. You bought our freedom with your suffering."

"So, we thought we'd better put it to good use," Helva put in. "We haven't been napping and eating pastries all this time. Well," she amended, "not *only* that."

"Indeed," Inga said. "This place may look exactly the same—which is not an accident—but you will find that the balance of power has shifted somewhat."

"You *have* been writing to Ursula," I realized.

"I did the actual writing," Helva informed me proudly. "I'm better at subtlety than Inga."

Inga made a face. "There is a time for subtlety and a time for assertive action." She turned her sharp turquoise gaze on me. "What is the rest of your plan?"

"I thought to rouse the women of the seraglio to take over the palace." When I said it, the plan sounded ill formed, full of holes, but Inga nodded.

"I'm glad to hear that my seeds have taken root," Inga said with a smug smile. "Everything is in place. I assume you plan to rally the women with your triumphant return, now that Deyrr has been defeated at your hands?"

I found myself gaping at her. "Is there anything you don't know?"

"If there is, my spies will pay for their lapse." She smiled with glittering resolve. "Go deal with Hulda. You'll save me doing it. I should warn you... You won't find her remorseful."

"Rather the reverse," Helva said with a grimace.

"Color me unsurprised," I replied, and we shared a moment, as we had over breakfasts, all those years ago when Hulda had ruled our lives with an elegantly jeweled fist. "I'm ready for her."

"Do you need back up?" Jepp asked, proving that she'd been listening all along. Excellent spying skills for a humble scout.

"No," I said. "This is something I need to do alone."

"Jepp and Karyn can help us spread the word among the ladies of your return," Inga said. "When you're finished with your mother, we'll pull the lever on our trap. I think you'll find it most effective."

I considered her. I didn't know if I'd given much thought to how Helva and Inga had spent the years, how they'd have used the freedom of unmarried women. Jepp had said she'd seen my sisters in Hestar's court, but I hadn't known how to credit that. "I feel rather less than an avenging rescuer now," I admitted with some chagrin.

Inga thawed at that. "Don't. Without your example, with what you did for us, we might not have thought to lay the groundwork for what will happen today."

Helva nodded, a harder expression on her pretty face. "Now we stage our revolution."

~ 16 ~

MY MOTHER'S APARTMENTS hadn't changed much either, except that they'd accreted layers of lavish decorations and treasures. She'd accumulated an amazing amount of stuff—but I supposed she had nowhere else to put it. Her wealth was borrowed, as women couldn't truly own property, so she had no option but to pile it into her apartments. As much power as she'd cultivated, it couldn't free her of the seraglio.

And clearly Inga ruled the women of the seraglio now—perhaps far more than that, given the hints she'd dropped.

Hulda's servants tried to stop me, but they crumbled before me, giving way as they would for a man. I used male command language ruthlessly, combining it with my imperial manners and the confidence I'd gained over the years. First Kaja had taught me how to handle myself, to rely on my sense of justice to step in where clear decisions were needed, and not to back down from bullies. Then Ochieng and the elephants had taught me the certainty of purpose. An elephant has no reason to heed the tiny human clinging to her back. Only knowing where I wanted to go, without wavering, could convince an elephant she wanted to go there, too.

I used all of that to scatter the servants and defenders of Hulda's apartments.

And ran smack into Hede.

She smiled with cruel vindication at the sight of me, her whip uncoiled and ready in her hand. "So, the rumors are true. Faithless Jenna, slinking home again. Did you think to regain your rank, your pampered life?"

"I want nothing from this place," I answered. Inside, Jenna stirred at the words, full of bloodthirsty rage. *It can be useful, if you're pointed at the right thing.* I slipped some of the control off my inner demon, carefully pointed her.

"That works out, because nothing is what you'll have," Hede sneered, cracking the whip. "You are nothing and no one now. What is more wretched than a woman who refuses her husband? You brought shame upon your mother, your entire family, and upon those of us who tried to raise you to be a decent wife." She flicked the whip, eyes hard. "I'm going to enjoy exacting punishment from that ugly skin of yours."

I laughed, giving her pause. "I suggest you get out of my way," I said pleasantly.

"You don't command me," she bit out.

"You're right, I don't. When I said I wanted nothing of this place, that included my rank. I have no wish to command you, but if you don't get out of my way, I *will* kill you."

She recovered fast, though not enough to completely cover her shock. "I'll be gentle this time," she sneered, "because you'll never escape again, and I'll want to enjoy whipping you for a long time."

Her whip cracked out, a strike for my face, to sap my spirit and perhaps scar me. When I'd been the treasured pearl of the empire, she hadn't been able to harm my pretty face. No surprise that she went for it first, a satisfying payback for the little restraint she'd had to exercise.

I dropped into a low lunge, drawing my daggers from the thigh sheaths—and fully unleashing Jenna from within. She let out a scream of rage, driving up and into Hede, who staggered back against the wall as one dagger drove into her gut and the other pressed up against her throat, shoving her jaw high.

Really, it was far too easy. "Drop the whip," I hissed.

Eyes rolling back in her head, she obeyed. "Not so simple, is it, Hede?" I asked sweetly, with syrupy sympathy. "You know how to whip children into obedience. How to threaten rekjabrel with disfiguring scars so they'll be cast out if they dare refuse being brutalized and raped nightly by the cruel men who call for them. You know how to force terrified and unwilling brides back to their husbands."

"It was my job, Your Imperial Highness," she stammered, shaking with real fear. "I was only doing my job."

"The weak excuse of the bully." I tsked, shaking my head, twisting the blade in her gut. She screamed weakly, already losing her strength. "I was there. You loved the paltry power you held over us. Over me."

"I was only enforcing the rules," she panted. "Please don't kill me. I'll serve you, in any way you wish."

"The world has no need of more bullies," I replied calmly. "I could make you suffer, for all those women who died under your whip, for all the ways you tried to break me. But I am not so cruel as you would've made me."

"Thank you, Princess," she sobbed. "I promise I'll—" She broke off in a gargle when I cut her throat, her worthless promises crumpling along with her body.

I looked down at the empty shell of her. "I lied," I said conversationally. "I was always going to kill you."

Stepping over her, I thrust aside the curtains, and entered my mother's inner sanctum.

She reclined, as she always had, on her mound of silk pillows, her opos pipe nearby. And, also as she always had been, she was impeccably groomed. Perhaps she'd been at court earlier, but that would be incidental. My mother had dressed herself to perfection every moment of her life, even in the middle of the night, always conscious of her duty to be ornamental. I'd never seen her not draped in an empire's wealth in jewels, without her beauty-enhancing makeup and elaborately styled hair.

At every moment, she lived and breathed being Empress of Dasnaria.

And she was beautiful. I'd forgotten the impact of her striking beauty—perhaps I'd thought my memories distorted by youthful admiration of the person who'd loomed largest in my life—but my travels through the world only reinforced how extraordinary my mother was. With jarring impact, I realized my mother was younger than Zalaika. And that when I left the seraglio forever, my mother had been younger than I was now.

She'd never lived outside this seraglio or the one she grew up in until she left at sixteen to wed the emperor. She was like this place, meticulously polished to present a perfect veneer, while beneath she was hollow. Corrupt, vile, ambitious, with no understanding of the vastness of the world, she was what they'd made her. What she'd tried to make me into. Had she ever loved me at all—or had she been incapable of it?

She looked me over, waiting pointedly. "Have you forgotten all of your manners along with your honor and duty?" she finally demanded. "Show me the courtesy my rank demands."

"I am," I replied. "You get no courtesy from me—and I bow and scrape to no one."

Her lushly painted mouth curled in an ugly sneer. "What have you done to your skin?" she demanded. "All those milk baths, all that effort to ensuring that your skin remained a pure smooth ivory, and what? You might as well have roasted yourself over a fire. I made you into a rare beauty and you threw it away to become this... awful *thing*."

"And hello to you, too, Mother," I replied, kicking myself for having wanted anything from her. Kaja and Zalaika had been truer mothers to me than this... wax doll had been. It was almost funny, how disappointing we found each other. Except it wasn't funny at all.

"You're covered in blood," she commented, gaze lingering on me with obvious distaste. "And where in the empire did you dig up that cheap, disgusting klút? You'll go bathe and change immediately. I'll send girls to do your hair and makeup. Maybe they can cover up some of that awful skin. I've made certain your rooms remained unoccupied and are ready for you, with plenty of proper klúts to choose from."

Of course she'd kept it all the same, the cage door invitingly open, should I be so foolish as to return. "I'm not here to primp, Mother," I said.

"Nevertheless, you will do it. No daughter of mine will be seen like that. Though I'm afraid nothing can disguise how you've let yourself go."

"I am not your daughter." As I said the words, the relief swept through me, more cleansing and refreshing than any bath. "You forfeited the right to call me that when you sold me to further your ambition."

"*Our* ambition," she snapped. "You always were a bit dense. Your father's blood, no doubt. Tell me, did you kill Rodolf?"

"Yes."

She nodded, unsurprised. "I thought you had that much of me in you. But you should have waited until you were installed in Arynherk. Your stupidity and frivolous defection stymied plans carefully laid for decades."

I'd known this, thought I'd understood her, but her obstinate focus on power above all still came as a revelation. "You didn't care at all what I suffered at his hands." Not a question.

She waved that off. "Bah. It's a woman's lot to suffer. Why should you be any different?"

"Because you were supposed to protect me." The words were angry, but a childish plaintiveness stirred beneath. I hadn't realized how betrayed I still felt. My mother had never been kind to me. She'd had me beaten to teach me lessons, had poisoned me so I'd understand the dangers of life in the seraglio, and had been exacting to the point of cruelty. But after all of that, I'd still thought she valued me in some way. And apparently fragile young Jenna still carried that inner pain of discovering that her mother hadn't cared about her at all.

"Protection creates weakness. I did better by you. I made you tough, strong enough to kill a weasel like Rodolf. Look at you now." She gestured to my bloodstained klút, sticking to me, it was so drenched. "I assume that's Hede's blood."

"Yes, I killed her, too."

"You always did bear her a grudge, and I don't blame you. I'm not angry. She'd outlived her usefulness anyway. Especially now that I have you." My mother studied me, then smiled. "I'm proud of you."

I'd once longed to hear those words. Now they turned my stomach. "For killing Hede."

"For the woman you've become, despite your ugliness—a real pity there—but look at you. Lethal. Cunning. Ruthless. You owe all of that to me." Satisfied, she drew on her opos pipe.

"I am who I am *despite* you," I replied steadily, feeling the truth of it. "And thanks to women who actually did care for me."

"Credit whoever you like. I'm not so weak as to need your mewling affection. Don't let it bother you that you turned out just like me. We'll make a powerful team because of that."

"Team?" I echoed, raising a brow, recognizing the cool contempt of the gesture as the same as Inga's.

"Yes. I have not been idle all these years. I have recruited powerful allies to repair the strategy you carelessly undermined." She gave me a falsely affectionate smile that made my skin crawl, though I was glad to find it no longer affected me as it once had. She had no idea, I realized, that Deyrr had been defeated. Inga and Helva had neatly cut my mother out of the communications web of the Imperial Palace, leaving her so isolated she hadn't even noticed her ignorance. A neat justice there, for the woman who'd worked so hard to make sure I knew only what fit into her use for me.

"You can be empress, Jenna," my mother said into my silence. "That fool brother of yours ran off, for a rekjabrel of all things, but you are firstborn, mine and Einarr's. It's time to reclaim your birthright. Remember what I taught you, the most important thing in the world?" Her jewel bright blue eyes hardened. "Power. And now at last it will be ours."

"You're wrong." I shook my head when she snarled at my impertinence. "Though you are right about one thing. The fact that you no longer have power over me does fill me with gladness. That's important. I'm sorry for your life, that you lived in a sunless room and were twisted into this monster who believes only power matters."

"Don't waste your pity. Power *is* all that matters. You are young and foolish still, to think otherwise." But she hesitated, looking me over, perhaps noticing the passage of time. Perhaps wondering if I had grown daughters of my own.

"That's not true. There's a whole world of more, Mother. There's love and—"

"Love is an illusion." She rolled her eyes, inhaling the opos smoke.

"Love is more real than power," I persisted, though I didn't know why. "Between people and between us and the animals of the world. The beauty of the sky, of sunrise and sunset, of the ocean and the grasslands—they stir the soul more than any jewel or embroidered silk ever could. There are people out there who are kind and help just because they can. People who protected me for no other reason than because it was the right thing to do. People who share their homes and food, because it gives them joy, because they know we aren't all dogs fighting over a bone."

"A bone!" She laughed at me, a harsh metallic edge to the once melodic voice, the bitterness inside leaking out. "With the power that I've resurrected, I will have all the world, and I will live forever."

"Resurrected?" I spun the dagger in my hand, drawing her unwilling eye. "Do you mean the High Priestess of Deyrr? I imagine she offered you immortality."

She regarded me with a hint of respect—and perhaps a glimmer of unease. "So you know about that. And it's no idle offer. I saw her mummified remains return to life with my own eyes, her eternal youth and beauty restored by the hand of the god."

"By your actions, you caused the deaths of thousands of people and horrible suffering for those who survived."

She drew on the opos. "What do I care for those miserable, meaningless lives? They are nothing to me."

"They are something to me, and to the goddess Danu. Her hand guides my blade and her clear-eyed wisdom guides the justice I bring to the source of the evil you unleashed upon the world."

She frowned, perhaps at last perceiving the danger. "It's not too late, Jenna. If you do as I tell you, I can find my way to forgiving you, and I will share this power with you. You, too, can be immortal."

"The High Priestess is dead, and Deyrr defeated."

"What do you say?" Her gaze stayed on my bloodied blade, understanding dawning at last. "That can't be."

"It can and is. I'm here to deal the final stroke of justice. Your death won't make up for all the deaths you caused, all the suffering you've wrought with your vanity, pride, and empty ambition. But it will keep you from hurting anyone, ever again."

"Jenna, wait!" She held out a hand. "Please, I—"

I threw the dagger, nailing her through her pretty jeweled eye—and she collapsed back, dead on the silk pillows.

"My name is Ivariel now," I said, and walked away.

~ 17 ~

THEY'D GATHERED ALL the women of the seraglio to sit around the big lagoon, Jepp stood guard over a small group that looked rebellious and sulky, including the charming Jasmyra. Two women in servant garb stood with her, apparently chatting companionably. Jepp caught my eye in question, and I nodded. She gave me a salute of sorts, fist over heart with a slight bow.

"She's dead," I told Inga and Helva, by way of greeting. Maybe I'd feel the reaction later, but at the moment I felt nothing at all, except a sense of resolution. I'd felt the same way knowing Rodolf was dead. Perhaps I was an unfeeling monster, made in my mother's image. "As is Hede. Any word from outside?" I was ready to leave this place.

Inga raised a brow, but didn't comment. "As you may note, not everyone is thrilled about our revolution." She waved dismissively at the group Jepp guarded. "We woke the children and moved them into Jilliya's old apartments, where they'll be safe with the elders looking after them. Word from outside is that Hestar accepted the *bjoja at haseti*. Loke is serving as Hestar's second and Harlan as Kral's. They were to engage in combat at any moment. I will receive word when they do. Odds currently favor Kral," she added.

Of course they did. Kral, the golden boy, could hardly fail. I looked to Jepp again. She had an ear cocked in our direction and a harsh look on her face. I wondered if she worried more about Kral losing to Hestar—or what would happen if he won.

"Your people are on the way to opening the seraglio," Helva added, sliding an inquiring glance at Inga.

"Yes, and our people are assisting them. I expect them at any time, so your speech will have to be short." Inga gestured to a raised platform. "Karyn found something for you to stand on."

"My speech?" I echoed.

"Yes, the rallying cry of the avenging angel. Inspire your troops, Sister."

I glared at Karyn as I made my way over, and she beamed back at me. "I hadn't planned on a speech," I told her.

"Did you have another plan for rallying them?" She sounded far too innocent.

I supposed I'd thought it would be like moving elephants, that I'd gesture and we'd charge. Just figured that people would be more difficult.

Karyn put a hand on my arm. "Tell them your story. If I hadn't known about you, I would never have had the courage to try to live in the outside world. Just give them your truth."

"I tried to tell my mother..." Ah, there was the emotion, grief tangled with a rage that might never fade. "She didn't listen."

"Maybe she couldn't hear it," Karyn offered. "When Jepp first offered me a way out, all I could hear was my own fear. Maybe if someone had offered Hulda a way out long ago, her life might've been different. It's too late for her, but it's not too late for these women. Not all of them."

"Thank you," I said. "That helps."

I stepped onto the platform, my bare feet remembering its smooth texture. I'd once danced on this, practicing the tight circles of the ducerse. Believing that perfecting the dance would give me everything I desired. Instead, I'd crawled through the broken pieces of myself to find what I hadn't known to want.

I'd found happiness. And that's what I'd brought back with me.

Looking out over the sea of faces—the wives, the concubines, the rekjabrel—I recognized some. Many I didn't. And yet, I needed to reach all of them. Another performance, but a critical one, to lead us all to freedom.

I summoned the dance, calling on Danu to guide not my feet or blade this time, but my words.

"Some of you remember me," I said, my voice carrying into the quiet, belling over the calm water of the lagoon. "Many may not have been here when I lived in this place, but you know of me. You've heard the stories. Now hear my truth. I was born in this seraglio, played among these ferns and palms. I grew up and lived among you for eighteen years as Imperial Princess Jenna. I lived the life of a Dasnarian woman, submissive, obedient, trained to serve the men who ran our lives.

"When I married—as I was told to do, to a man known for his violence and brutality—I suffered greatly at his hands. Some of you will remember that, too." A number of the women averted their gazes, some faces creased in sympathy, others in hard commiseration. "It is a woman's lot to serve, we've been told, whether it gives us pleasure or pain. A woman's lot to suffer, some say. I'm here to tell you that is a lie. This life, this place, the cake you eat, is all a lie." I swept my hands at the false tropical paradise, sunk deep beneath the lake.

"I'm here to tell you the truth: I escaped that marriage." A murmur ran through them, some faces alighting with vindication, others dubious. "I escaped Dasnaria. I took a sailing ship across the sea to a city where women roam freely, where they handle money and own property, and only marry if they wish to—and they choose who to. They choose who they take to their beds, and do so for their pleasure, for love, for happiness."

I spun into a movement of the ducerse, blades flashing. "I learned to use the dances of my youth to wield blades, to defend myself and others. My journeys continued—for the world is larger than anyone can imagine—and I went to the hot grasslands of another land. I became Ivariel, warrior priestess of Danu. I fell in love with a man who has never raised a hand to me in twenty years of joyful marriage."

The murmurs grew louder. "I have four children, and I have a herd of elephants who fill my life. It is a wide, glorious world, and I'm here to tell you that you do not have to live in this seraglio any longer."

"But it's dangerous out there," a woman shouted, a rekjabrel I recognized.

"Is it?" I demanded. "More dangerous than the men who use you? So many of us die at their hands, from violence and from neglect. How many years do you have left in you, Mara? The world offers you the chance to take care of yourself, where you don't need to be anyone's ornament or sexual servant." I looked at Karyn, sheathed my blades and held out a hand to her, helping her up onto my platform. "Karyn has been there, too."

"I have," she said, too quietly, then lifted her chin and her voice. "I was afraid, certain I would die without the protection of my husband, my father, my brothers. With no one to feed me, how would I eat? With no bed to warm, what shelter would I have?"

The women nodded, a murmur of agreement washing over us. "But I found those things for myself." Karyn stabbed a finger at her chest. "I have fought in battles, and I have taken a lover for joy of being with him. And I came back here to fight for *you*, so that you may have the same. You do not have to live this life any longer."

"They treated us like children to be kept under watchful eye," I added. "But we are women grown, and the world belongs to us as much as it does to men. It's time to leave the seraglio and walk the earth as adults."

As if on cue, a booming sound hit the doors. Something clattered on the other side. The doors shivered. Women squealed and I held up my hands to calm them. "Those are our liberators," I explained. I hoped.

Another *boom!* And the doors shuddered in their frame. "Today we tear down these doors!" I shouted. "They have been the locked gate that kept you in this cage. If you wish, you may still live in here, but you will come and go at will."

Boom! The doors shattered, pieces falling inward, revealing two huge grizzly bears in the frame. Women shrieked—and my own heart clutched at the terrifying sight—but Karyn let out a glad cry and ran toward them.

The twin bears disappeared, becoming Zyr and Zynda. Zyr caught Karyn in his arms, kissing her long and deep, then tenderly wiping her tears away. The room fell silent at the sight. He looked up, scanning the scene. "Good Moranu," he said. "This is worse than the zoo at n'Andana."

She laughed a little, and Zynda came up to us, bringing with her a slender, dark-skinned man with solemn, intelligent eyes and a long queue of deep brown hair. He nodded at Inga and Helva. "Everything is in place, Your Imperial Highnesses," he said with a bow. "Several carts of weapons await at the top of the stairs." He turned to me, bowed again. "You must be Priestess Ivariel. I am Akamai, a friend of Queen Dafne Nakoa Kau'Po." He winked. "Librarian and spy, at your service."

"I'm glad to meet you," I said, then looked between him and Zynda. "Kral's status?"

"Hestar is faltering, but Leo is leading the guard to surround them. It sounds like they have orders to cut down Kral and Harlan if Kral is victorious. The situation does not look promising."

At those words, Jepp blazed past at top speed. Karyn looked at Zyr. "My bow is on top of the tower we came in."

"Let's go get it," he replied, and became a huge black cat. She climbed astride, and he galloped up the stairs with her.

"Ivariel?" Zynda asked. I hesitated, looking to Inga and Helva.

"Go with them," Inga told me. "Go protect Harlan." She and Helva exchanged a fierce look. "We'll lead the women to take the palace from within."

"Will they know how to use the weapons?" I asked.

Inga beckoned to the servant women Jepp had been talking to. "This is Sunniva and Runa. Jepp taught them how to turn everyday tools such as scissors into weapons. Every woman who wished to learn has been taught." The two women curtseyed deeply.

"It's an honor to meet the lost princess," Runa said.

"You are our hero," Sunniva agreed with a shy smile.

"Jen—I mean, Ivariel, is a hero to all of us," Inga said. "You are right, Ivariel. I respect who you've chosen to be. That was an excellent speech," she added with a smile, and Helva fanned herself.

I seized her, and Helva, in a tight embrace—remembering the last time, when we said goodbye. "I'll see you soon," I promised.

"It better be sooner than twenty years!" Helva shouted at my back. Zynda had become a tiger, glorious and terrifying in her fiery beauty as she pranced impatiently waiting for me. Hers was a beauty my mother could never have understood, much less hoped to match. I hesitated only briefly, then clambered astride, her fur velvet soft and inches thick. She took a few experimental steps, and I clung with my thighs.

"I'm good," I said. "Run like the wind."

~ 18 ~

ZYNDA RACED AFTER Jepp, who'd been passed by Zyr and Karyn. She ran gamely on down the hallway—and I saw Karyn standing outside the open door of the room we'd come in.

"To the roof," she called, and I shot a fist in agreement. Good plan. We burst into the room and Zyr, in gríobhth form, stood on hind legs, front talons gripping the window ledge. Dawn was breaking outside, soft rose and gold breathing against the violet blue, lovely and unconcerned about the pitched events of the mortal creatures below.

Zyr spun his glossy black eagle's head around and clacked his lethally curved beak impatiently at Karyn. "I had to wait to tell them, didn't I?" she bit out, vaulting onto his back.

No sooner was she in place than he gathered his haunches and sprang out the window—dropping like a stone. With a choked cry, I ran to the window, only to be nearly blown back by the furious wings of Zyr shooting to the top of the tower.

Zynda flew past me in hummingbird form, then burst into her enormous dragon self in mid-sky.

"Guess we're done being subtle," Jepp observed, pointing past Zynda to Kiraka diving with billowing flame. She disappeared beyond the curve of the walls—to where we'd last seen Kral and Harlan.

"Guess we're climbing up," I said, my shoulders weeping at the thought as I clambered onto the window ledge.

"Guess again," Jepp called, right as Zynda's taloned dragon hand reached out and plucked me from the ledge.

Yes, I screamed, before I managed to quell the animal terror. She held me in her scaly palm, the claws making a cage to keep me from falling. This kind of cage I didn't mind a bit. Zynda circled once, then swept down to pluck Jepp from the ledge. She handled it much better than I had, leaping with agile grace and finding purchase, clinging to one huge talon. Presumably she had some practice with this sort of thing.

Maybe when we got back to Annfwn, I'd put Jepp on Violet—or Efe!—and see how she did then. Then Zynda rounded the curve of the palace walls and all frivolous thoughts fled from my mind.

Hestar had cheated, indeed. I didn't know much about how the men arrayed their forces, but I did know enough of the epic sagas to recall the rules of the *bjoja at haseti* and it was absolutely supposed to be single combat, no interference. Not this.

Men in armor—they did look like a cavalcade of black beetles from this height—streamed across the single bridge over the lake, joining a deep circle surrounding the fighting pair and their seconds. Jepp seemed to be studying the bridge with great interest, and I realized all the drawbridge sections were down, making a single, unbroken surface. It made sense on one level, not to slow down reinforcements heading out—but it also would make it easier for an army going in.

Too bad we didn't have an army.

Zynda passed over the incipient battlefield, giving us a good look, then roared at the men running across the bridge. They screamed, diving off into the water, and I felt much better about myself for being scared. More guards streamed in from the outposts around the lake—or they tried to. Kiraka dove at them, fiery breath making them flatten to the ground. Marskal, atop Kiraka's back, gave Zynda a fist-pumping signal, then pointed Kiraka to burn arrows out of the air that shot toward Zyr and Karyn, who flew in from the far side.

Karyn had her bow strung, quiver on her back, but she didn't fire on anyone. Our side, at least, respected the *bjoja at haseti*. Theirs seemed to be close to breaking it, which meant we'd face the all-out battle we'd hoped to avoid.

Harlan guarded Kral's back, holding off the encroaching circle of warriors testing his defenses. They mostly feinted, to my eye, preparing to cut him down the moment either Kral or Hestar failed. Which looked to be soon.

My two brothers circled each other in the clearing of armed warriors, both visibly exhausted. Their plate armor hung off here and there in jagged pieces, and Kral was dragging one leg. Hestar still wielded his broadsword with both hands, but it sagged to one side, where the shoulder was clearly injured. He shouted something and charged Kral, swinging that mighty blade and connecting with Kral's side, the *clang!* so loud it echoed up to us. The assembled men cheered, and Kral staggered drunkenly.

In Zynda's other fist, Jepp stood poised with vibrating tension, glaring daggers at the duel as if she could affect the outcome with her gaze alone. If I'd ever doubted the realness of the love between Jepp and Kral, I didn't anymore. And I also understood how and why that love had changed him.

Love had changed me, too. So many people had offered love to me without reserve or price. Perhaps we weren't all doomed to become what our parents had been—and what they'd tried to mold us into. And all because Harlan had refused to go along with things as they'd always been. He'd dared to defy them all— and lit a spark for a fire that kept spreading.

"Drop me next to Harlan!" I shouted up to Zynda.

Jepp's head whipped around, then she nodded. "Me too."

Zynda dropped, swooping low over the lake of armored warriors, arrows bouncing off her scales with chimes like music. She held us carefully protected, then backwinged sharply as the ground rushed up.

"Drop and roll!" Jepp shouted. I nodded. First thing we taught the kids on riding elephants—how to fall off. Zynda opened her dragon hands, giving me a slope at least, and I tumbled down it. I hit ground with a decent roll, and came to my feet behind Harlan.

"Your sword's on my belt," he said, keeping his own pointed at the men edging ever closer.

"Thanks. Inga and Helva say hi."

He grunted, lifting his sword menacingly at a warrior who took a step. "And Hulda?"

"Dead."

"Good. Any of that your blood?"

"Nope."

Another soldier abruptly jolted forward, scrambling back when Harlan swung his sword with a roar.

"This looks bad though," I commented, moving my sword to loosen my shoulders, twirling the dagger in my other hand.

"You think?"

"Worse than you know. Reinforcements are pouring in from the back. These guys are getting pushed from behind. Soon they'll figure that out and break ranks."

"You sure you don't know battle strategy?"

"I never said that. I know plenty about fighting aggressors— just not beetle men."

He laughed, a short bark. "How'd the duel look?"

"Like two drunks reduced to taking blind swings. I can't tell who will fall first."

"Either way, we'll be swarmed the moment one does."

"Looks that way."

"Whoever thought up this plan is an idiot."

"Sounds like my Kral," Jepp said, rejoining us, a dagger in each hand. "My question is, since Hestar already cheated, and we're all doomed either way, why can't I kill him?"

"Because Hestar is mine," I said. "Remember your prophecy?"

"Right. Yeah." She rolled her eyes. "Too bad you didn't summon a bigger army of dragons, shapeshifters, and sorcerers, though."

"Didn't I? I think it's time to call Andi."

Her eyes widened. "Danu's tits, you're a genius." She grabbed me and kissed me hard on the mouth. "Go slay that monster. We'll have your back."

Jenna boiled up in me, and I welcomed her fury. The blood burned hot in my veins, creeping red-black in the corners of my vision. The red rage, indeed. I lifted my sword.

"Hestar!" I bellowed, striding forward. As I passed Kral, he collapsed to his knees, and Jepp rushed to his side, helping him up, and dragging him toward Harlan's shielding sword.

Zyr landed in whoosh between their trio and the advancing guard. He screamed an unearthly eagle's cry and lion's roar at them, and the men scrambled back in terror. Karyn leveled her bow at them. "First man to move gets an arrow in the eye," she snarled at them.

Hestar stared at me as if seeing a ghost. Good. I smiled.

"Hestar, son of Einarr," I shouted. "I am your elder sister, Jenna, and I have come to take your life."

He actually took a staggering step backward, his face inside his helm pale, his eyes bright with fear. "Jenna?" he managed.

"The very one. The gods are disappointed in you, Hestar. You betrayed Sól by allowing Deyrr into your heart and mind. You have been stripped of your divinity."

"You're not Jenna!" he shouted. "Jenna is dead."

"That's right." I smiled, letting Jenna shine through with her bloodthirst. "I died. I died a thousand deaths, and now I've come from the afterlife to drag you back with me. Time to die, Hestar."

He threw down his sword, and ran.

Laughing, I ran after him. He was pitifully slow in his heavy armor, already exhausted from battling Kral. I caught up and leapt, kicking him hard on the back of his knee, sending him to plant his face in the ground. He began crawling, sobbing, calling for someone to save him.

Behind me, dragons roared and people shouted. The sky seemed to be suddenly filled with sound and fury.

I ignored it all, stalking on silent bare feet after the pitiful Hestar. Reaching him, I put the point of my sword at the weak join between helm and the carapace of armor over his shoulders.

"Will you die face down in the mud like a worm?" I inquired silkily. "Or will you be a man and face your death?"

He rolled over onto his back, flinching when I put a foot on his chest, pinning him down. His pale blue eyes watered in his puffy face, and he held up empty mailed hands in a plea. "Please. Jenna, please! I'll give you anything. Wealth. Power."

"I don't want those things."

"What do you want? We were close once. They called us the twins, remember? We can be close again."

"There is one thing I want," I conceded.

"What? Anything."

I lifted my dagger hand, showing him the thick scars ridging my wrist. "I want this to have never happened. I want all my scars, inside and out, to be gone. Can you do that for me?"

He gaped. Stammered. "I... I'm sorry that happened."

"Are you?" I inquired as if casually curious. Something roared overhead with a blaze of heat and Hestar stared in horror. I didn't bother to look. "Pay attention, Hestar. A man only dies once. You should be present when it happens."

"I would've helped you if I could have, Jenna" he protested.

"Jenna is dead," I replied. "You helped murder her."

"I couldn't do any—"

I stabbed my sword through his open mouth. "Liar," I said softly.

He reached up as if to grab the blade, but already the life faded from his eyes. They fell to the ground as he died.

I turned to face the rising sun and began a dance of prayer, repentance, and gratitude.

~ 19 ~

THE NOISE AND fury of the attack turned out to be largely illusion—though one powerful enough to scatter the Imperial Palace guard into the forest. Zynda and Kiraka drove off the few brave men who tried to take a stand. Zyr and Karyn picked off the rest who attempted to fight.

Kral mustered the ones that remained, who threw down their arms. These men had served him as General of the Dasnarian forces. With Jepp fierce and bloody at his side, Kral organized the guard, detailing a group to carry Hestar's body into the Imperial Palace.

"We'll burn him according to tradition," Kral informed us as we joined him. Andi's illusions had faded from the sky. Kiraka, Zynda, and Zyr making lazy sweeps to patrol the blue sky of a lovely summer morning. "It's more than he deserves," he said, face lined with exhaustion.

"But it's the right thing to do," Harlan agreed. "If we're not going to burn the empire down, then we should observe the order of things."

I snorted at that, and both men grimaced. Leo and Loke stood under guard nearby, glowering. Mykal was indeed out at sea with the navy, and Ban was apparently at a country estate where he was taken care of. I looked from our angry brothers to Kral. "So."

He shook his head. "Technically you won the *bjoja at haseti.*"

"He surrendered, and I killed him anyway. That was vengeance, not a challenge of honor," I replied. "You made the challenge and would have won."

Kral shook his head. "I never wanted to win." He looped an arm around Jepp, leaned heavily on her. "I have no desire to be emperor," he said to her, then grinned at us. "Good distraction, though, huh?"

Jepp muttered something under her breath, but she held him up. Harlan looked at me. "Do we call you empress now?"

"No." I saw it very clearly. "Jenna was firstborn, perhaps a monster molded in her mother's image, but she died. I am Ivariel, with no right or desire to sit on the Dasnarian throne."

Harlan nodded, unsurprised. Kral cast a dubious glance at Leo and Loke. "From what I've seen of the terror twins, neither is a good candidate."

"I know who it should be," I said. When I followed the men carrying Hestar's body into the palace, the others followed behind me.

Inga met us at the door. A brace of women, and some men, all bloodied and looking fierce with it, flanked her. Helva stood at Inga's side, and gave a glad cry when she saw me. Inga nodded, clearly pleased to see us well, but somber at the sight of Hestar's body. She lifted her clear eyes to me in question.

I went down on one knee. "The emperor is dead," I told her. "Long live Empress Inga."

Behind me, Kral and Harlan echoed my gesture, shouting the same words. Helva dropped into a deep curtsy, chiming in. Gradually, the word spread through the people inside and out of the palace, the shouts gathering volume and conviction. Dragons adding a bass roar, the higher notes of Zyr's eagle scream threading through like the golden sunshine.

"Long live Empress Inga! Long live Empress Inga!"

IT TOOK US a while to sort everything out. Harlan and I guarded Inga as she asserted control of the Imperial Palace, the Domstyrr, and the reins of an empire. Helva and Akamai worked furiously on the documentation—with priority on the edicts to withdraw the navy. Inga's second Imperial Decree granted women full rights as citizens and ordered all seraglios be unlocked.

It would take a while to enforce, but it would happen eventually in every corner of the empire.

Jepp took Kral to the infirmary, where he promptly passed out and she sat over him in worried vigil. She did, however, identify former High Priest Kir when he was unearthed from the entertainment salons. Marskal and Zynda volunteered to take him to Annfwn—which they did, trussed and tossed over her shoulders along with a few other bags—and they returned the next day with Ash, who set to healing Kral. They also brought me my own clothes, and letters from Ochieng, Ayela, and my kids, which I read with much weeping, as if I hadn't seen them for a hundred years.

I attended the ceremonial burning of Hestar and Hulda. And we used the remnants of the seraglio doors for kindling on their funeral biers. Harlan, Kral, and I said the official prayers for them. When I spoke the words, I said them for my young self instead, finally laying Jenna to rest.

Jepp and Kral decided to stay a while, to help Inga consolidate her hold on the throne, though Jepp wryly commented that they would *not* be staying long, she didn't care how free the women were. Zyr and Karyn stayed, too, though they did plan to journey soon to the Hardie estates. Inga asked if they'd help distribute the news of women's emancipation throughout the empire as well, and they'd both agreed.

Prince Fredrick and Princess Ada also arrived, immediately pledging fealty to Inga, and eagerly jumping into plans for reform.

As for us, we went home. Harlan and I flew to Annfwn on Zynda, and once again I sat between Marskal and Harlan. It had only been a few days, but I longed to see my family.

As the sea smoothed and became tranquil, turning into a clear aqua like Inga's eyes, my heart rose. I'd washed myself clean of the blood and death, leaving it all in the funeral ashes we'd scattered in the lake around the Imperial Palace. I'd left Jenna behind as well, the lightness inside me bearing witness that the heavy coil of her rage and hatred had at last been excised.

The white cliffs of Annfwn rose up—and I spotted elephants playing in the gentle surf. Zynda winged into a landing, and I climbed down with much more practiced ease, hurrying because I'd spotted Ochieng and the kids racing down the beach toward us. Ochieng reached me first—but only because Ayela and Kajala hung back, grinning at each other. My husband caught me up in a fierce embrace, kissing me deeply. In the familiar heat of his mouth, the strength of his arms, I had returned home.

"I thought you might be tempted to stay," he said, laying his cheek against mine.

"Never. My home is with you."

He pulled back to study my face. "You look good," he decided. "Happier. I think you've never been lovelier."

And I knew he meant it, because he truly loved me, and those eyes see the clearest of all.

TITLES BY JEFFE KENNEDY

FANTASY ROMANCES

A COVENANT OF THORNS
Rogue's Pawn
Rogue's Possession
Rogue's Paradise

THE TWELVE KINGDOMS
Negotiation
The Mark of the Tala
The Tears of the Rose
The Talon of the Hawk
Heart's Blood
The Crown of the Queen

THE UNCHARTED REALMS
The Pages of the Mind
The Edge of the Blade
The Snows of Windroven
The Shift of the Tide
The Arrows of the Heart
The Dragons of Summer
The Fate of the Tala
The Lost Princess Returns

THE CHRONICLES OF DASNARIA
Prisoner of the Crown
Exile of the Seas
Warrior of the World

SORCEROUS MOONS
Lonen's War
Oria's Gambit
The Tides of Bára
The Forests of Dru
Oria's Enchantment
Lonen's Reign

THE FORGOTTEN EMPIRES
The Orchid Throne
The Fiery Crown
The Promised Queen

CONTEMPORARY ROMANCES
Shooting Star

MISSED CONNECTIONS
Last Dance
With a Prince
Since Last Christmas

CONTEMPORARY EROTIC ROMANCES
Exact Warm Unholy
The Devil's Doorbell

FACETS OF PASSION
Sapphire
Platinum

Ruby
Five Golden Rings

FALLING UNDER
Going Under
Under His Touch
Under Contract

EROTIC PARANORMAL

MASTER OF THE OPERA E-SERIAL
Master of the Opera, Act 1: Passionate Overture
Master of the Opera, Act 2: Ghost Aria
Master of the Opera, Act 3: Phantom Serenade
Master of the Opera, Act 4: Dark Interlude
Master of the Opera, Act 5: A Haunting Duet
Master of the Opera, Act 6: Crescendo
Master of the Opera

BLOOD CURRENCY
Blood Currency

BDSM FAIRYTALE ROMANCE

Petals and Thorns

OTHER WORKS

Birdwoman
Hopeful Monsters
Teeth, Long and Sharp

Thank you for reading!

About Jeffe Kennedy

Jeffe Kennedy is an award-winning author whose works include novels, non-fiction, poetry, and short fiction. She has won the prestigious RITA® Award from Romance Writers of America (RWA), has been a finalist twice, been a Ucross Foundation Fellow, received the Wyoming Arts Council Fellowship for Poetry, and was awarded a Frank Nelson Doubleday Memorial Award. She serves on the Board of Directors for the Science Fiction and Fantasy Writers of America (SFWA) as a Director at Large.

Her award-winning fantasy romance trilogy *The Twelve Kingdoms* hit the shelves starting in May 2014. Book 1, *The Mark of the Tala*, received a starred Library Journal review and was nominated for the RT Book of the Year while the sequel, *The Tears of the Rose* received a Top Pick Gold and was nominated for the RT Reviewers' Choice Best Fantasy Romance of 2014. The third book, *The Talon of the Hawk*, won the RT Reviewers' Choice Best Fantasy Romance of 2015. Two more books followed in this world, beginning the spin-off series *The Uncharted Realms*. Book one in that series, *The Pages of the Mind*, was nominated for the RT Reviewer's Choice Best Fantasy Romance of 2016 and won RWA's 2017 RITA Award. The second book, *The Edge of the Blade*, released December 27, 2016, and was a PRISM finalist, along with *The Pages of the Mind*. The final book in the series, *The Fate of the Tala*, released in February 2020. A high fantasy trilogy, The Chronicles of Dasnaria, taking place in *The Twelve Kingdoms* world began releasing from Rebel Base books in 2018. The novella, *The Dragons of Summer*, first appearing in the *Seasons of*

Sorcery anthology, finaled for the 2019 RITA Award.

Kennedy also introduced a new fantasy romance series, *Sorcerous Moons*, which includes *Lonen's War, Oria's Gambit, The Tides of Bàra, The Forests of Dru, Oria's Enchantment, and Lonen's Reign*. And she released a contemporary erotic romance series, *Missed Connections*, which started with *Last Dance* and continues in *With a Prince* and *Since Last Christmas*.

In September 2019, St. Martins Press released *The Orchid Throne*, the first book in a new romantic fantasy series, *The Forgotten Empires*. The sequel, *The Fiery Crown*, followed in May 2020, and culminates in *The Promised Queen* in 2021.

Her other works include a number of fiction series: the fantasy romance novels of *A Covenant of Thorns*; the contemporary BDSM novellas of the *Facets of Passion*; an erotic contemporary serial novel, *Master of the Opera*; and the erotic romance trilogy, *Falling Under*, which includes *Going Under, Under His Touch* and *Under Contract*.

She lives in Santa Fe, New Mexico, with two Maine coon cats, plentiful free-range lizards and a very handsome Doctor of Oriental Medicine.

Jeffe can be found online at her website: JeffeKennedy.com, every Sunday at the popular SFF Seven blog, on Facebook, on Goodreads and pretty much constantly on Twitter @jeffekennedy. She is represented by Sarah Younger of Nancy Yost Literary Agency.

jeffekennedy.com

facebook.com/Author.Jeffe.Kennedy

twitter.com/jeffekennedy

goodreads.com/author/show/1014374.Jeffe_Kennedy

Sign up for her newsletter here.

jeffekennedy.com/sign-up-for-my-newsletter

Made in the USA
Monee, IL
15 September 2020